woul

The n

LONDON

D0528723

Dear Reader,

Thank you for picking up a copy of *Unwrapped by the Duke*.

London, England, has always been a destination at the top of my bucket list. I've been in love with everything British since I was a young girl and was forced to watch countless hours of *Fawlty Towers*, *Monty Python* and *Blackadder*. 'Forced' is not the right word... I highly enjoyed spending that time with my father, and it started my lifelong love of anything British.

My love for and fascination with the British monarchy stems back to that magical moment when I was only five years old and I stayed up to watch Princess Diana marry Prince Charles. I was in a sleeping bag on the floor, staring up at the television in wonder and awe.

I had so much fun writing about Thomas Ashwood, Duke of Weatherstone. He was a delightfully dark and delicious hero to write about—although he has a hard time believing in love after a very lonely childhood. Dr Geraldine Collins comes from a very different world from Thomas's—but only different in situation. She's also had a very lonely childhood, with a cold, detached mother and a father she doesn't know exists until the start of our story.

Thomas and Geri don't believe in love. They think they're fine on their own—until they meet and realise just how lonely they both are. I hope you enjoy Thomas and Geri's story just as much as I enjoyed writing it.

I love hearing from readers, so please drop by my website, amyruttan.com, or give me a shout on Twitter @ruttanamy.

With warmest wishes,

Amy Ruttan

UNWRAPPED BY THE DUKE

BY

AMY RUTTAN

MILLS & BOON

Published in Great Britain 2016
By Mills & Boon, an imprint of HarperCollins*Publishers*
1 London Bridge Street, London, SE1 9GF

© 2016 Amy Ruttan

ISBN: 978-0-263-91524-2

Our policy is to use papers that are natural, renewable and recyclable
products and made from wood grown in sustainable forests. The logging
and manufacturing processes conform to the legal environmental
regulations of the country of origin.

Printed and bound in Spain
by CPI, Barcelona

Born and raised just outside Toronto, Ontario, **Amy Ruttan** fled the big city to settle down with the country boy of her dreams. After the birth of her second child Amy was lucky enough to realise her lifelong dream of becoming a romance author. When she's not furiously typing away at her computer she's mum to three wonderful children who use her as a personal taxi and chef.

This book is dedicated to my Aunt Margaret. She is the one who got me interested in everything to do with the British Royal Family. She sent me books, newspaper articles, magazines. Thank you, Aunt Margaret. So glad you shared your interest with me.

This book is also dedicated to my dad, who set me on the path to loving anything British or British comedy-related. So, Dad, and the rubber button is…?

Praise for
Amy Ruttan

'Amy Ruttan delivers an entertaining read that transports readers into a world of blissful romance set amidst the backdrop of the medical field. Sharp, witty and descriptive, *One Night in New York* is sure to keep readers turning the pages!'
—*Contemporary Romance Reviews*

'I recommend *Perfect Rivals*… as a place to start for those who haven't thought of trying the Medical line before, because this will be an absolute treat… I give it five stars because of the characters, the plot, and the fact I couldn't put it down… Please read this book— *stat*!'

—*Goodreads*

'The secrets, the rivalry and the electrifying chemistry… *His Shock Valentine's Proposal* is a treat for fans of Medical romances!'
—*Goodreads*

CHAPTER ONE

"AND THIS IS WHERE you can change into your lab coat while you make rounds on our patients."

Geri nodded her head as she followed her father into the lounge all the surgeons and physicians at the hospital used. There were overstuffed sofas and a sparkling kitchen area. It was a comfortable enough room, more than comfortable, a lot different from the rooms in the inner-city Glasgow hospital where she'd done her residency. Those rooms usually had a couple of vending machines and a ratty old settee. Not that she'd spent much time in the doctors' lounge. She'd spent most of her time on the surgical floor.

Until a month ago when she'd given up her chance to be a surgeon.

She'd had every intention of finishing her surgical residency, but circumstances had changed after her last year on rotation and her father's offer to become a cardiologist had suited her just fine.

She'd been surprised at the opulence she found herself suddenly thrust into.

Of course, her father was a prestigious cardiologist, with a practice in Harley Street. Being a member of the peerage, he was used to working in more comfortable surroundings.

She was finding it all a bit overwhelming.

It had only been last year that her estranged father had

reached out to her and she'd gone from that young girl who'd grown up in a poorer district of Glasgow, studying hard to get scholarships and working two jobs to pay her way through medical school, to heiress.

Geri had spent her whole life doing everything in her power to make a better life for herself, to distance herself from her cold, detached mother who was now living in some commune in Israel. A mother who had no interest in a connection with her daughter anymore.

Which also suited Geri just fine.

So it had been a complete shock to her system to finally meet her father and find out that he was an aristocrat—a lord—and that she was a lady and the heiress to a family seat that stretched back to the time of King George III. And it wasn't just that. Her father was retiring and he was leaving his practice to her.

When he'd offered her the practice last year she'd turned him down. She'd been involved with Frederick and on her way to becoming a cardiothoracic surgeon.

Besides, she hadn't really wanted to get to know the man who hadn't given two figs about her existence until it had suited him.

Then Frederick had broken her heart and because of her relationship with him she'd became the laughing stock of the surgical program in Glasgow. She'd decided to take the easy way out and take her father up on his offer.

A secret shame she'd have to bear. Which was only fitting punishment for thinking herself in love with a surgeon she'd been learning from. For letting her emotions rule her heart.

Her mother had told her time and time again to hide away her feelings. Feelings served no purpose. They were a form of weakness.

So she'd left Glasgow for London to take over her father's share of the practice.

Surgery was the price she had to pay for her indiscretion.

It wasn't a solo practice, as her father shared his practice with a cardiothoracic surgeon, but that didn't matter. It's what made her father's practice one of the top ones in Harley Street. In the same office you could meet with your cardiologist and one of the best cardiothoracic surgeons was just down the hall. Geri had yet to meet the infamous Mr. Ashwood, but she had read some of his research papers when she'd been doing her surgical residency. He was certainly an impressive and accomplished surgeon.

"Geraldine, you looked a little flustered. Are you sure you're well, my dear? We can save this walk-through for another time. You've only just arrived from Glasgow. Perhaps you should go back to my house and unpack. Rest."

"No, I assure you I'm fine." Geri smiled. "Please do continue."

She couldn't bring herself to call him "Father" just yet. He was still Lord Collins to her. She was staying at his home for now. Just until after Christmas when she could find her own place. It was awkward, to say the least. He walked around her like she was delicate china and was going to shatter.

They'd been together for a month and she felt like she didn't even know him. And she wasn't all that sure she wanted to.

Her father nodded, though he looked uncomfortable. Sometimes it was hard, being alone with him. It was awkward. They were too polite, but then there were other times when they enjoyed each other's company. Still, those times were few and far between.

He looked down at his pager. "Ah, a spot of trouble. One of my patients has just been admitted. Would you like to come meet her or would you rather stay here?"

"I'll stay here, I think. Just get my bearings. I'm sure I'll meet her soon enough."

Her father nodded. "I won't be a moment."

Geri breathed a sigh of relief when her father left her alone.

She was still trying to process it all. She couldn't quite believe she was here. It had always been a secret dream of hers to meet her father one day. Until each year had passed and those secret dreams of her father coming to rescue her from a lonely childhood had faded into nothing. At the age of eighteen she'd had his last name, known his first name was Charles, but had had no idea that he was a member of the aristocracy. And she couldn't be bothered to find out anything about him.

She'd had no idea he was a physician in Harley Street with a home at the posh end of Holland Park.

It was all a bit overwhelming. She sat on the edge of a couch and took a deep breath.

What am I doing here? I don't belong here.

"Excuse me, but are you lost?" It wasn't totally a question. It was a question mixed with annoyance.

Geri stood and turned around. She was taken aback by the tall, dark, handsome surgeon standing in the doorway, his face like thunder as he glared at her, letting her know in no uncertain terms she didn't belong there.

"Thank you for your concern, but I'm not lost."

He cocked his head to one side. "This room is for surgeons only. I think you're in the wrong place."

His voice was deep and husky, which sent a shiver of anticipation through her. She always fell for dark, brooding men. Frederick had been dark and brooding and look how that turned out.

Don't get carried away.

"I can assure you I'm not lost," she said again. "I was accompanying my father and he asked me to wait here until he returned. Besides, this is the physicians' lounge. Not the surgeons' lounge."

He snorted and moved past her into the room. "I'll have to have a talk with them, they'll let just about anyone in here."

"My, we're in a foul mood, aren't we?" She was tired of pompous, arrogant, rude people.

He poured himself a cup of coffee and then turned to look at her. "You're not from around here, are you?"

"Oh, and what was it that gave it away?"

He grinned. "That delightful accent you have. Somewhere in Scotland, I assume."

He was right, of course, but she wasn't going to let this holier-than-thou surgeon off the hook. He was presumptuous, conceited and haughty. And handsome, but never mind that. He needed to be taken down a peg or two.

"You know what they say about assumptions," she muttered under her breath.

He crossed his arms and leaned back against the counter, his eyes twinkling. "No, what do they say? Enlighten me, miss."

Darn.

He'd heard her. Well, two could play at this game.

"It's 'Doctor,' actually," she said, correcting him.

He cocked his eyebrows. "Is it really? Are you going to be working here, then?"

"In a manner of speaking." She tried to be evasive and end the conversation with him, but she wasn't that lucky. The way he'd asked if she was going to be working here made her feel nervous. Like suddenly she was a mouse and he was a cat, closing in for a kill.

He grinned, a lazy sort of grin that Geri knew all too well from the rogues she was used to dating. That smile was wolfish, almost predatory in nature, and as he set his coffee mug down and moved away from the counter towards her, Geri knew she was in deep, deep trouble.

"Well, my apologies, then. I had no idea that you were a new surgeon here."

"Just a doctor, actually. I'm not a surgeon." It stung to say that, but she didn't let it show. Her mother couldn't tolerate any show of emotion and she had learned well.

"I just naturally assumed you were a surgeon. You have an authoritative air about you."

"And only surgeons have the right to be authoritative?"

"Yes. I mean, lives are in our hands."

Geri rolled her eyes. Good lord, he was arrogant. "You're unbelievable."

"Why, thank you." He made a bow with a flourish.

"It's not a compliment. You're the most conceited, prideful man I have ever had the displeasure of knowing."

"Oh, come, now, darling. Surely not the worst?" He winked. "You've only known me for a few fleeting moments. Spend some more time with me and you'll no longer feel displeasure."

"Don't call me darling. I'm most definitely not your darling."

He leaned over and whispered in her ear, his hot breath fanning her neck, "Ah, but you could be."

It took all her strength not to slap him hard across the face or let him kiss her. It had been a long time since Frederick. A long time since she'd felt any kind of desire for a man.

"Geraldine, I'm sorry I took so long," her father said, coming into the room. She jumped back, silently thanking her father for his timing. "Ah, I see that I no longer have to seek you out, Thomas. Geraldine, I would like you to meet Mr. Thomas Ashwood. Thomas, this is my daughter, Geraldine Collins. She'll be taking over my position in the practice when I retire."

"Pardon?" Thomas said, sounding a bit dumbfounded. He was sure he'd heard the enchantress say the same thing the moment Charles Collins had dropped the bombshell on him. "What was that?"

"My daughter, Dr. Geraldine Collins. She's the cardiologist who is taking over my role in the practice. She'll be your partner."

Oh. God.

He'd been hitting on Charles's daughter? His competition, the bane of his existence since Charles had announced that he was retiring and leaving the practice. Thomas had thought that he was going to take over the practice in its entirety. He'd planned to hire an up-and-coming cardiologist and expand the surgical side of the practice. Take it to new heights, ones that he'd never been able to meet before.

But now he found himself with an unwanted new partner. The daughter of the great Charles Collins. He knew the type. Debutante. Spoiled, selfish and she would be all over him in a trice when she learned of his aristocratic background. Society women were out for money and blood.

It was all the same with women from the circles he moved in and he'd expected nothing different from Collins's daughter.

Until now.

She was nothing like he'd expected. She stood up for herself. She exchanged banter with him and didn't back down. He liked matching wits with someone. Not only was she a beauty, she was intelligent to boot. It was kind of exciting and also a bit bothersome. To her credit, Dr. Geraldine Collins didn't look exactly thrilled at the prospect of being his partner either.

"This is Mr. Ashwood?" Geraldine asked. Thomas couldn't help but notice the mild disgust in her voice. "This is *the* Mr. Ashwood who is your partner in your practice?"

Thomas bowed slightly at the waist. "One and the same, dear lady."

Geraldine's eyes shot daggers at him.

"Have I missed something?" Charles asked, apparently confused.

"No, nothing at all, Charles. I didn't exactly make my presence known to your enchanting daughter when I arrived. I'm afraid I took her a bit by surprise."

Charles Collins cocked his eyebrows. "Oh. Well, that explains everything."

"Aye?" Geraldine blushed and cleared her throat. "I mean, I suppose it does."

Thomas had been charmed the moment the "Aye" had slipped past her lips. She seemed refined, but she had obviously not been raised in the world he was used to, the world that both he and Charles came from.

And that intrigued him all the more, which was a dangerous thing indeed. He had to make an expeditious exit or he might do something he'd regret. And he thought too highly of Charles to besmirch the good name of Collins.

"Well, if you'll both excuse me..." As he was trying to make his excuse his pager and Charles's both went off. It was their patient, Lord Twinsbury. He was on his way to hospital and E.

"Blast," Charles said. "I have an office full of appointments."

"I can handle this, Charles," Thomas offered.

"I can assist," Geraldine said to her father. "You can head back to the practice and I can assist Mr. Ashwood."

No.

"That's an excellent idea," Charles said. "You met Lord Twinsbury last week when he visited. You're familiar with his file. What say you, Thomas? I mean, you'll eventually have to work together when I retire officially, so why not take the plunge now?"

"I don't think I'll need Dr. Collins's assistance in this matter." He was grasping at straws, but he really needed to get away from Geraldine. She piqued an interest in him that he hadn't felt in some time and he didn't like the way it made him feel.

"With all due respect, Mr. Ashwood, we don't even know if this is a surgical case," Geraldine said firmly. "And I *will* be present as we both examine Lord Twinsbury."

She had spirit. He liked that.

"You don't have hospital privileges."

It was a weak excuse.

"I do, as a matter of fact. I was granted them this morning." Geraldine crossed her arms, smiling very smugly.

"Now, instead of standing here and arguing, why don't we meet Lord Twinsbury in A and E and give him the attention he needs?"

Thomas was stunned as Geraldine moved past him and headed out into the hall. Even Charles looked a bit shocked but Thomas didn't have time to sit there and hash it out with him. Instead, he ran to catch up with Geraldine, who was marching away, her back ramrod straight and honey-brown strands of hair escaping that severe bun that was pinned at the back of her head. He couldn't help but admire her backside as she marched down the hall.

Don't think about her like that. She's off-limits.

"Do you even know where the A and E department is?" Thomas asked as he fell into step beside her.

She rolled her eyes at him. "Don't be silly. Of course I do."

"Good, because right now you're headed to the operating theater floor and A and E is this way." Thomas motioned over his shoulder in the opposite direction. He should've just let her go and get lost. Then he could deal with Lord Twinsbury himself, only something deep inside him, that nagging conscience he tried so often to ignore when it came to the opposite sex, was yelling at him to do the right thing.

She skittered to a stop and looked down the hall, her

hazel eyes sparkling with determination, annoyance and possibly embarrassment, her red lips pressed together in a firm line.

"Are you going to show me the right way, then, or am I to find the way myself?"

"If I was going to let you fend for yourself I wouldn't have stopped you and told you were going in the wrong direction."

Geraldine's shoulders relaxed and a small smile crept onto her face. "Thank you. I didn't think you would… That is to say…"

"There's no explanation needed." Thomas knew what she was trying to say, that she didn't think he would help her, and part of him was telling him not to. To let her flounder. She was, after all, the competition. Only he couldn't do that.

He might go by "the Dark Duke" in his social circle, the rake who seduced debutantes and left them the next day, but he was, after all, a gentleman above all else. Only, since the moment he'd first begun arguing with her, he'd been trying not to think about all the ungentlemanly things he wanted to do to her.

"It's this way," he said, motioning with his head.

She nodded and they walked side by side down the hall, not saying a word. He was truly impressed that she was able to keep up with his long easy strides in her tight pencil skirt and heels.

She was graceful, refined, but there was something hidden beneath that polished, emotionless surface. Something quite different from the women he was used to. She was tough, hardened but he had no doubt she was soft and feminine under that facade. He would like to find out, she intrigued him.

But he would not seduce Charles's daughter and since

settling down was out of the question for him, he would just have to keep a safe distance from Geraldine Collins.

They entered A and E and were waved over by the consultant in charge.

"He insisted on having his cardiology team come and look at him," Dr. Sears said, looking over at Geraldine, confused, before turning back to Thomas. "Where is Dr. Collins?"

"I am Dr. Collins." Geraldine pushed past him and Thomas shrugged, smirking. He had to admire her tenacity.

Lord Twinsbury was quite pale and lying back on the gurney. He smiled, though, when Geraldine came in.

"Ah, I thought I would be seeing your father but I assure you this is a better substitute."

Geraldine smiled. "Lord Twinsbury, you're a flirt."

"How many times do I have to insist you call me Lionel?"

Thomas cocked his eyebrows. Never in the thirty-odd years he'd known Lord Twinsbury personally and the five years he had been the man's surgeon had he been permitted to call him Lionel.

And Lord Twinsbury was one of his godfathers.

"Lionel, then." Geraldine smiled. "What seems to be the matter?"

Lord Twinsbury craned his neck and looked at Thomas. "Young fellow, they paged you as well. That's good."

"I would certainly hope that they would page me as well, my lord, or perhaps you'll allow me to call you Lionel, as well?"

Lord Twinsbury fixed him with a stare, much like his own dear departed father used to do. "I think not. You're not an attractive lady, like Geraldine is."

The stern smile softened as he looked over at Geraldine, who was taking Lord Twinsbury's blood pressure and frowning.

"Look at this, Mr. Ashwood," she said. Thomas leaned over to look at the reading and grimaced.

"Well? What's wrong? I can tell by your faces that my blood pressure isn't good."

"No, it's not, my lord." Thomas pulled out his stethoscope. "Do you mind if I have a listen?"

Geraldine helped Lord Twinsbury sit up as Thomas listened to the erratic sound of Lord Twinsbury's heart trying to pump blood through his clogged arteries. He had been warning Lord Twinsbury for years that his clogged arteries would only get worse. They had done several angioplasties at different times, but Thomas knew and had told him that one day it would come to open heart surgery.

It looked like that day had come.

"I can tell by your face, Thomas, that you're going to tell me something I really don't want to hear," Lord Twinsbury said.

"You can call me by my given name but I can't call you Lionel?"

"Your father would have a thousand fits knowing you're being so informal with me," Lord Twinsbury warned.

Thomas rolled his eyes. "My lord, you know what has to happen. I've told you this day would come. You need a coronary artery bypass graft and you need one today. Now. Or the next time you're speaking in the House of Lords you're liable to drop dead."

Geraldine gasped. "You have a terrible bedside manner, Mr. Ashwood."

Lord Twinsbury chuckled and patted Geraldine's hand. "Nonsense. I'm used to his behavior. I like his frank talk, my dear. It keeps me on my toes."

Geraldine frowned and Thomas winked at her.

"I'll have you admitted, Lord Twinsbury, and then we'll get you ready to go up to the operating theater today."

Lord Twinsbury nodded and then turned to Geraldine.

"I do hope you'll stay, my dear. Your father has been treating my heart for so many years and I want to make sure I have someone I can trust in there."

Thomas groaned and walked out of the room.

Lord Twinsbury was an eccentric character. He was also pompous and arrogant. Never took his advice. Probably because he still saw Thomas as that little boy who'd destroyed his Tudor hedge maze during Royal Ascot when he was ten.

"Mr. Ashwood, can I speak with you a moment?"

Good. Lord.

His day had been going so well. He'd done a great LVAD surgery to extend the life of a patient and was planning on returning to his office to get some charting done. He had not planned to deal with Charles Collins's daughter today.

He turned around. "How can I help you, Dr. Collins?"

"Do you treat all our patients in such a manner?"

"I do, as a matter of fact, because most of them I've known for quite some time. I haven't had any complaints yet."

"Do you think that he warrants a coronary artery bypass graft? Wouldn't another angioplasty or perhaps an endocardectomy work in this case? Is surgery really the answer for a seventy-three-year-old man in poor health?"

This was a little too much.

"Have I missed something, Dr. Collins? Are you or are you not a surgeon?"

Red tinged her cheeks and he'd hit a tender spot on her hardened walls. A chink in the armor, as it were. So perhaps there was a weakness, a crack in her icy facade. "I am a cardiologist so, no, I am not a surgeon."

"Then do not question my surgical opinion."

"Lord Twinsbury is as much my patient as yours."

"Your father would never question my surgical decisions," Thomas snapped.

"Perhaps he should."

Thomas took a step closer to her. "How long have you been treating Lord Twinsbury, Dr. Collins? A few hours, perhaps. I have been treating him for five years and over that five years I've done numerous angioplasties and made a failed attempt at a carotid endocardectomy, which almost killed him. I have informed my patient that he would need a coronary artery bypass graft. I have tried to keep the procedures as minimally invasive as possible for the sake of my patient, who has been in congestive heart failure for a long time, but there is no other option, so unless you're able to perform in the operating theater and have discovered a new, minimally invasive way of doing a coronary artery bypass graft, I would suggest you head back to our surgery in Harley Street and leave the surgical procedures to the qualified individuals."

He turned on his heel and left her, hating himself for taking her down like that in the hallway, in front of the A and E department and other physicians. Physicians she'd be working with.

He hated himself for making her feel that way.

If it had been anyone else, he wouldn't feel as bad as he did now. He'd given dressing-downs like that before and they had never eaten away at his conscience, but this was different.

He didn't know why, but it was and he didn't like it one bit.

CHAPTER TWO

I SHOULD LEAVE.

Geri bit her lip as she paced the viewing gallery of the operating theater where Thomas Ashwood was currently performing a coronary artery bypass graft on Lord Twinsbury. How she wished she could be in there, assisting. She'd read so many papers Mr. Ashwood had written. A few hours ago she would have given anything to learn from him.

Now she knew that would be a mistake. Just like Frederick had been a colossal mistake. She was here to start afresh. To prove herself. There was no way she was going to become entangled in a dalliance at work because the last time it had cost her her surgical career.

It didn't have to.

Geri shook that thought away and closed her eyes, thinking about the surgery and how she wished she was in that operating theater. Only Mr. Ashwood had made it perfectly clear that he did not want her around.

She'd been embarrassed and after her temper had cooled she'd realized he was right. She wasn't a surgeon; she may have seen and done surgeries during her residency, but she wasn't a full-fledged surgeon and she never would be. Besides, she'd only known Lord Twinsbury for a week and even though she read over his file she hadn't worked with him as long as Mr. Ashwood had.

She wanted to apologize to him.

"Apologizing is a sign of weakness."

Geri shook her mother's voice from her head. Apologizing in this case was not a sign of weakness but respect. She'd been wrong.

Geri had been less than thrilled to learn that the arrogant, pompous surgeon who had come sweeping into the doctors' lounge, making assumptions about her, was her new partner. And she'd been taken a little off guard by the fact that he was a devilishly handsome, well-spoken man of breeding. As well as a surgeon she admired.

Which meant he was completely off-limits.

Definitely.

She had been hoping that she wouldn't have to see him again, but to find out that he was the cardiothoracic surgeon and partner in the practice was too much to bear. She'd been expecting Mr. Ashwood to be someone like her father. Older and possibly on the verge of retirement.

If Mr. Ashwood was venerable she'd eat her hat and try to find out where he kept the youth elixir. She couldn't help but wonder what her father saw in him. Her father only seemed to associate with those of his own class, members of society, what would've once been affectionately referred to as "the *ton*" if all those historical romance novels she'd read as a girl were correct.

She had been surprised to see her father's partner was someone so young and his complete opposite. Her father was reserved, awkward and well-bred. Mr. Ashwood had a relaxed, devil-may-care attitude. A definite rogue. Then again, her father had partnered with her mother, a common daughter of a Glasgow teacher, and had produced her.

Yeah, but that didn't last too long, did it?

Geraldine paused in her pacing to look down at him,

operating on Lord Twinsbury. Even in the operating theater he had a commanding presence and she couldn't help but admire his technique. She may not be a surgeon, but she'd watched many surgeries and Mr. Ashwood knew exactly what he was doing and he was doing it with finesse.

"There you are, Geraldine."

Geri turned to see her father enter the observation room.

"I thought you went back to the office?" she said.

Her father shrugged his shoulders. "I was going to, but then I heard a rumor that Thomas gave you quite a dressing-down in the hall."

Heat bloomed in her cheeks. Great. She was already making the rumor mill here. She swallowed her pride. "And rightfully so. I stepped out of line."

"I should say so." A smile played on her father's lips and she couldn't help but smile secretly to herself. He was still handsome. Even at sixty-nine she could see why her mother had fallen for her father. Or had at least stuck around long enough to conceive her.

She just didn't see what her father had seen in her mother.

"I'm hoping he'll allow me to apologize to him," she said, rubbing the back of her neck.

"It's best not to bring it up. Don't let him see your soft underbelly. You gave an opinion, and though not the right one, it was still an opinion nonetheless. Thomas is ruthless. It's why I asked him to be a partner. He's talented but ruthless. If you want to survive in a successful practice with him you have to stand by everything you say. You have to bite back."

Geri cocked an eyebrow. "Bite back?"

Her father nodded. "It will blow over and you'll both find a rhythm of partnership. So why don't we head home? I had Jensen bring the car around."

Even though she was sorely tempted to leave and not

expose her soft underbelly to Mr. Ashwood, she couldn't leave things like they were. She had been wrong to question him.

And she wasn't going to run this time. She was here for the long haul.

"I think I'll stay if it's all the same to you."

"Are you sure, Geraldine?"

She nodded. "Positive."

Her father reached down and squeezed her shoulder. "Just call for the car when you need it, then. Jensen won't mind."

"Of course."

Only she wouldn't. She'd take the tube to Holland Park. She may not be from London, but she knew her way around public transportation just fine. She just wouldn't tell her father that. He would have a thousand fits if he knew that she was taking public transportation like a commoner. Only that was what she was.

She may talk in a refined way, because she worked hard to drop the rough accent she'd had since childhood, but she didn't belong in this world she'd just been thrust into.

The first time she'd had a formal dinner at her father's large Holland Park home she'd been so confused by the number of forks she'd made an excuse about not being hungry and had left the table.

Her father had been less than thrilled to find that she'd walked down the street to the local pub and had had something to eat there.

What am I doing here?

She tried to tell herself that she was getting to know her estranged father, taking the opportunity of a lifetime of inheriting a lucrative practice in Harley Street, but she wasn't sure that was it.

There was a buzz on the intercom, snapping Geri out of her reverie. She got up and pushed the button.

"Dr. Collins, I'm surprised to see you up there," Thomas said, not looking up at her.

"Well, Lord Twinsbury did mention that he wanted me close by."

Thomas glanced up and there was a twinkle in his eyes. "So he did. Why don't you scrub in and come down here? You can keep me company."

"I thought since I wasn't a surgeon my place wasn't in the operating theater."

He chuckled. "So I did, but I think this once I can make an exception for my new partner. Will you come down?"

"I'll be right there." Geri let go of the buzzer and made her way down to the change room, where she found some scrubs. A nurse led her to the scrub room, where she scrubbed down and then entered the operating theater. She kept a discreet distance so she didn't contaminate the sterile field. She'd missed being in the operating theater. It had been so long.

"I wanted to apologize, Mr. Ashwood," she said.

"Whatever for?" he asked absently, in that haughty way that drove her insane.

"I think you know."

He shook his head. "No apology needed. I might've been too harsh on you. You're allowed to have an opinion."

Geraldine was shocked. Frederick would've never admitted that to another surgeon or doctor.

"I really think—"

"No. It's done. More suction, please." Thomas didn't look at her as he continued the surgery. "Lord Twinsbury is a friend of my father's. I've known him for quite some time. I get a little overprotective of him."

"I see. Is your father friends with my father?"

Thomas smiled behind his mask, she could tell by the way his eyes crinkled. "No, in fact they were nemesis… or is that nemeses?"

Geri chuckled. "Rivals?"

"In some respects," Thomas said. "Although my father was not in the medical profession. I believe they were both rapscallions in their youth. Playing the field and going after the same women."

Geri's stomach twisted in a knot and she had a hard time picturing her father as a rapscallion. "Is that a fact?"

"Yes. I was surprised when your father brought me on when I completed my surgical residency. He had the most prestigious cardiology practice in Harley Street and I was willing to give my eyeteeth to work with him. I had to convince him that taking on a surgeon was a good business decision."

That was more believable. In the short time she'd known her father she'd gathered he wasn't one to take chances.

"Well, you seemed to have won him over."

"He never told me about you, though, not until a couple of months ago when he said you were joining us." This time he looked up from the surgery to fix her with those dark eyes that seemed to see past her facade into her very soul.

"My father and I don't have the best relationship. Or at least we didn't. I'm hoping to rectify that now." She hoped he didn't know she was lying through her teeth and under his hard stare she felt a bit uncomfortable.

"You're not even listed in *Debrett's*."

"Should I be?" Geri asked, hoping her voice didn't rise with her nervousness.

"Your parents were legally married."

"Briefly. I believe the divorce was finalized just after I was born. My mother left before she knew she was pregnant with me."

"So you should be in *Debrett's*, given that your father has a seat in the House of Lords."

"You seem to know a lot about me."

"I know nothing about you and that's the problem." He held out a hand while a scrub nurse passed him an instrument. "You're a complete mystery."

"Why are you even looking me up in *Debrett's*? What does it matter if I'm listed in there? It's a pretty useless publication, if you ask me." She crossed her arms, hugging herself, as if that would hide the fact that she was the estranged daughter of an aristocrat.

She'd read this story a million times in the romance novels she cherished. Only those novels were fiction and fantasy. This was real life.

And she was a doctor, a darned good doctor who was specializing in cardiology, and she had no interest, at the moment, in anything beyond medicine and helping her patients.

"It is that," Thomas agreed. "I mean, who needs to know who is thirty-seventh in line to the throne?"

"Exactly. I don't know and I really don't care."

"So what do you care about?" he asked.

"Medicine. It's all I care about."

He chuckled and shook his head. "You should've been a surgeon."

"And why is that?"

"You're cold. Detached. Vicious."

"I'll take that as a compliment," she said.

"I meant it as one," Thomas said. "But surely you have some interest beyond medicine. Reading, travelling…crochet?"

"Crochet?" she asked, trying not to laugh at the absurdity.

"It's good for the hands. Keeps the fingers strong and the mind sharp."

"Do you crochet, then?"

"Good lord, no."

"Then who told you that crocheting keeps the fingers strong and the mind sharp?"

"My grandmother, but then again she was a bit batty."

Geri couldn't help but smile. "So what do you do, then?"

"I paint."

Now she was intrigued. "What do you paint?"

"Nudes mostly." And he waggled his eyebrows at her over his surgical mask. She couldn't help but laugh along with the others in the room.

Frederick would never joke like this.

It was beneath him and Geri found herself liking this laid-back camaraderie. There was a light in the darkness of a serious surgery.

"I read a study once that said patients, although under general anesthesia, are aware of what is going on around them. Subconsciously. Better outcomes when the surgeon is happy."

Thomas stared at her and she regretted opening her mouth. Was he going to berate her again?

"I heard that too. And I believe it." He returned to his work and Geri watched him. Thomas was just as impressive as she'd always thought he would be.

Thomas laid down his instruments. "Dr. Fellowes, would you close up for me?"

"Yes, Mr. Ashwood." Dr. Fellowes stepped into the lead surgeon spot and began to close up the patient.

Thomas moved past her to the scrub room and Geraldine followed him as he peeled off his gloves, mask and surgical gown, placing them in the receptacle, before he began to scrub his hands.

Geraldine did the same.

"That was textbook surgery, if I do say so myself." There was a smug, satisfied smile plastered across Thomas's face.

"I'm glad it went so well."

"Well, the surgery went well. The next twenty-four hours will tell me the entire picture." Thomas dried his hands. "It's still touch and go. Recovery will be the key to success or failure."

"Will I see you tomorrow at the office?" Geri asked.

"No," he said. "I plan to stay close to Lord Twinsbury tonight. I will be monitoring him in the intensive care unit."

"Is it because he's a family friend or do you do that for all your patients?" She was teasing, she didn't really expect such a high-class surgeon to remain by his patient's bedside. Especially an elderly one like Lord Twinsbury, who, given his health, probably wouldn't have much of a shot of pulling through.

"All of them. Every last one."

She was stunned and was positive her mouth was hanging open by the way he grinned at her.

"Have a good evening, Dr. Collins."

Geri watched him walk down the hall. She shook her head. Every time she tried to fit Mr. Ashwood into a certain slot in her mind, he completely and utterly didn't fit.

And just as she'd surmised before, he was a danger.

A very sexy, tempting danger that she wanted no part of.

"You took the tube again didn't you?"

Geri hung up her coat on the coatrack in her father's office. "Well, you didn't wake me when Jensen took you to work."

"You got in late. I thought you'd appreciate the lie-in."

She had actually. "Yes, but today is clinic day. How am I supposed to get to know my new patients if I spend half the morning in bed?"

"Why didn't you call Jensen to bring you in?" her father asked. He sounded tense, as if he'd been worrying about her the whole time. Which was nice, but unwarranted. She was an adult.

"The Westway is jam-packed or didn't you hear about that?" she asked.

"Jensen could've taken the Bayswater Road. The Westway is always jam-packed at this time of day."

"I'm quite used to taking public transportation."

"I know, Geraldine, but your situation is different now." He returned to his work.

She took a seat in front of her father. "And how is it different? I still am the same person and no one knows me from Adam."

"You're a lady of means. An heiress," he said, not looking up.

Geri wrinkled her nose. "I'm a doctor."

Her father ran a hand through his hair and then sighed. "You're just as stubborn as your mother."

Geri shrugged. "I'll take that as a compliment." Though she really didn't think it was much of a compliment as she didn't want much association or comparison with her mother.

"Hmm." Her father then pulled out a cream-colored envelope and handed it to her. "You've been invited to your first social gathering."

She took the envelope and stared at the fancy calligraphy. "What's it for?"

"It's for a party after the London International Horse Show. We've both been invited. It's formal attire as the Duke of Weatherstone has been invited. You know he's in the line of royal succession."

Geri cocked her eyebrows and stared at the invitation. "How do I turn it down?"

"You can't turn it down."

"Why not?" she asked, flipping it over. "It's for this weekend."

"And what plans do you have for this weekend?"

She shrugged. "Christmas shopping."

"You're going. I've already told our hostess we'd be attending. Besides, it's a good way to get to know some of our patients. A lot of them will be there."

Before she could argue there was a knock at the door and Thomas stuck his head in. There were dark circles under his eyes, as if he'd been up all night, but that didn't deter from his general svelte and put-together appearance.

Good lord, he was handsome and a brilliant surgeon to boot.

Why did he have to look so good?

He's off-limits. Off. Limits.

"Am I interrupting?" Thomas asked.

Yes.

"No, Thomas, come in," Charles said.

Thomas opened the door and came in, jamming his hands in his finely tailored trouser pockets. "I wanted to report that Lord Twinsbury made it through the night."

Her father nodded and smiled. "That's excellent news."

"Wonderful," she said.

Thomas glanced at her briefly, his gaze landing on the cream-colored envelope. "Ah, I see the invitations for the Gileses' party have arrived."

"Yes, apparently the Duke of Weatherstone will be there," Geri teased.

A strange look passed across his face. "Well, I can tell you who won't be there—Lord Twinsbury. He'll still be in hospital for another week at least. At least he's out of the intensive care unit, but he's demanding to see his cardiologist."

Her father sighed. "I'll get Jensen to bring the car round."

"No, Charles. He wants the good-looking one." Thomas grinned at her. "He's asking for you, Dr. Collins."

Her father chuckled. "You'd better go, Geraldine. And please take Jensen."

"The Westway is completely jammed, though," Thomas said. "She could always take the tube."

Geraldine couldn't help but laugh at that, especially when her father glared at Thomas. "Only if you accompany her."

"Of course. I am a gentleman after all."

"That remains to be seen," her father mumbled.

Geraldine set down the invitation and grabbed her coat, heading out into the hallway with Thomas.

"So much for getting to know patients today." Geraldine followed him down to his office, where he grabbed his own coat and wrapped a scarf around his neck.

"You are getting to know a patient by going to the hospital and attending Lord Twinsbury. By doing so you're letting your other future patients know that you care."

"He just had surgery, you should be the one attending to him. Not me. I'm not the surgeon."

Which was a bitter pill to swallow.

"And I will be. I am accompanying you after all." Thomas cocked a head to one side. "You're not wearing a hat?"

"No, should I be?"

Thomas shrugged. "It's cold outside."

"I'm from Scotland. This is not cold for December. This is balmy," she teased.

"Balmy?"

"Yes. Exactly."

Thomas just shook his head. "Come on, then, my lady, I'm to be your escort to the tube."

Geri fell into step beside him and they walked down the street toward Regent's Park Underground Station.

"You know, it's been some time since I've taken public transport," he said offhandedly.

"Don't tell me you have a driver as well."

"Good lord, no. I find it a particular challenge to wrestle my way along the motorways on my daily commute."

"You're an interesting character, Mr. Ashwood," Geri remarked. "Wrestling motorways and painting people in the nude."

"Oh, yes, which is why you should get to know me better," he whispered huskily.

"Hmm, that remains to be seen."

"You still never told me what interests you beyond medicine, Dr. Collins."

"I do like reading."

"I do hope it's racy novels."

"Naturally," she teased, completely forgetting herself. *What're you doing?*

"Actually, I love Jane Austen."

"Most ladies do. I prefer Chaucer myself and Icelandic skalds."

"You're a man of many hidden depths."

"I could say the same about you, Dr. Collins. Except the man bit."

"I think since we're going to be partners you can call me Geri."

He cocked an eyebrow. "Geri? No, I think I'll call you Geraldine."

"Why? Only my father calls me Geraldine. No one else calls me Geraldine."

"Except me. Now. Geraldine. I like the sound of it. It's elegant."

"Hardly. I always hated the name."

"You shouldn't. It suits you."

"So what do I call you?" she asked.

"You can call me Thomas."

"Not Tom?" she teased.

"If you expect me to answer, no."

"You're so frustrating." Geri walked ahead of him. "I don't need an escort to the hospital."

She was hoping that he would take the hint and head back to the practice, only he didn't. He kept pace with her.

"Go back to the practice, Mr. Ashwood."

"I'm hurt. What happened to using our given names?"

"You became pedantic and annoyed me," Geri said, but a smile hovered on her lips. She was enjoying herself immensely. Which was a bad thing.

"I've been called many things, annoying especially, but never pedantic. That's a new one."

Geri couldn't help but laugh as they headed down to the underground at Regent's Park Station. When they were on the tube, crammed close together as they rode in silence, Thomas glanced down at her.

"Why don't you like Geraldine? It's a lovely name," he asked.

A hot flush crept up her cheeks. No one had ever called her name lovely before. She'd always hated it. Men would usually call her Geri. Geraldine was an old-fashioned name.

"I thought I'd name you Geraldine after your father's mother since that's the only thing you'll be getting from him."

Of course, Geri had never met her namesake.

"It's an old-fashioned name." It was an excuse. She did like her name, but preferred to be called Geri. When she'd learned Geraldine was a connection to her long-absent father who had never come to rescue her, she'd wanted to cut that tie.

She'd learned the hard way that she could rescue herself.

He shrugged. "So is Thomas, but I quite like it. Geri makes you sound like a singer in an all-girl pop band."

She laughed. "Well, I like Geri."

"And I like Geraldine. You'll see it my way soon enough

and you'll be begging me to say your name over and over."
His voice was deep, like thick honey. Honey, which she
pictured smearing over his body and licking off.

Blast.

"Are you propositioning me?"

He grinned, a smile that was dangerous and made her
feel weak in the knees. "And if I was?"

"I would tell you to keep looking." She turned her back
on him, but couldn't help but smile. It had been a long time
since a man had flirted with her. When Frederick left her,
no one had had anything to do with her. It had been as if
she'd been a pariah.

And she'd known there had been a rumor going around
that she was a cold fish in bed. Unfeeling. And that could
be true. She'd never particularly liked sex. Yet when
Thomas flirted with her, her pulse quickened and her body
reacted to being so close to him.

He had some kind of spell over her. He was so tall,
standing next to her on the tube, that longish dark hair
styled so fashionably, the twinkle to his eyes and saucy
smirk on his mouth. He was so confident.

She'd forgotten how much she liked the attention and
she wished she had half the confidence and appeal he
was oozing.

Don't think like that.

She wasn't going to get sucked in. She wasn't going to
let another man affect her. This was her chance at something great. Geri was going to prove that she earned this
partnership, just as much as she'd inherited it.

And nothing was going to get in her way.

CHAPTER THREE

THOMAS STOOD IN the hall, watching Geraldine with Lord Twinsbury. Before they had got to the hospital Lord Twinsbury's vitals had dropped and he'd had to remain in the ICU for the time being, but as he watched Geraldine talk with their patient, he could see color coming back into the old coot's cheeks.

And he couldn't help but grin. Geraldine may be a bit cold with him, but with patients she was gentle and kind. She had a good bedside manner. Even with Lord Twinsbury, who was a tyrant. Just like his own father had been. Tyrants didn't faze her. She held her own and he had to admire her spirit. She was strong. Stronger than any woman he'd ever known.

Most women in his circles wanted to be saved or acted helpless at times.

A dressing-down would've outraged them, but it hadn't bothered Geraldine one bit. In fact, she'd admitted her mistake and apologized.

It took a lot of gumption to do that. Now she was in there with Lord Twinsbury and handling him as if Lord Twinsbury was nothing more than a gentle kitten.

Which was far from the truth.

Lord Twinsbury had been as much of a reprobate as his father and Lord Collins had been. Thomas knew who the woman his father and Lord Collins had fought over was. He was staring at her daughter. He had been seven at the time, he just didn't know all the particulars.

His father had been widowed for three years and had been looking to find love again. His father had never talked much about the woman he'd been trying to woo, had said only that Lord Collins had come out from under him and swept the woman off her feet.

And it had always been a point of contention with his father that Geraldine's mother had chosen Lord Collins over him. His father had become bitter, even more so, and Thomas had resented that woman for making his father miserable. Of course, that hadn't worked out well for Geraldine or Lord Collins either.

He'd done research last night, checking on Lord Twinsbury, and that research had been Lord Twinsbury actually telling him a thing or two about what had happened.

Although Lord Collins had been head over heels in love with Geraldine's mother, the two had come from two different worlds and had not been suited. She had been a friend of a friend and had gate-crashed a party his father and Charles had both attended. And both of them had been enchanted by her. Apparently Geraldine's mother was cruel, emotionless, and had crushed Charles's heart.

Charles had never known until recently that his short-lived marriage had produced a daughter. According to Charles, his ex-wife had left not knowing she was pregnant and hadn't bothered to tell him she was carrying his child.

Thomas couldn't even begin to imagine the pain that must've caused Charles.

For Charles may have been a rascal and rogue in his younger halcyon days, but he knew Charles had suffered from an unimaginable heartache. He knew that Charles was trying to do his best to bridge the gap between him and Geraldine.

Only Geraldine was not meeting Charles halfway and he couldn't help but wonder why.

Thomas loved his father, but his father had always been a bit too distant, a bit bitter, and Thomas had spent most of his childhood at boarding school. He knew that his father had had a hard time looking at him because it had reminded him of his dearly departed wife. Thomas had had a lonely childhood, deprived of love.

"Ah, 'what tangled webs we weave,'" Thomas muttered under his breath.

You should keep moving. Stop staring at her.

Only he couldn't help but stare at her.

Unlike his father, he had never had his heart torn apart by grief, although he had experienced a disastrous infatuation in his youth. A woman who had been more interested in the title he was to inherit. The social status. She hadn't loved him for himself.

"Why do you need to work as a surgeon? Your family has enough money and land. Why not run your estates?"

"Cassandra, that's not what I want. I love medicine. I love surgery and saving lives is my passion."

She had never understood him. Not really, and he'd been blinded by lust. Then his father had died of undiagnosed hypertrophic cardiomyopathy and Thomas had found out he had the genetic predisposition for it too. He'd decided then and there that family was not for him. Especially when he'd seen how small a comfort Cassandra would be should the worst happen. Suddenly, to her, he had been defective. A lesser being. Being alone was far better.

Was it?

He shook his head in disgust with himself.

He'd only been around Geraldine Collins for a day and she was getting under his skin. He couldn't allow her to do that.

You can seduce her. You are after all the Dark Duke.

Maybe if he had her once it would purge her from his system.

What am I doing?

He ran a hand through his hair. He was actually standing outside a patient's room and contemplating seducing the estranged daughter of his colleague, a physician he truly admired. When had he become so jaded?

But he knew the answer to that.

"Lord Twinsbury seems to have stabilized," Geraldine said, coming out of ICU and disposing of her gown and gloves. "What is your assessment, Mr. Ashwood?"

"I think he should stay in the intensive care unit for now. The last time I thought his condition had stabilized, we prepped him to take him out of the ICU and his stats took a dive. It's better he stay here for now. There's no rush to move him."

Geraldine nodded. "Well, I've done all I can here. I think I'll head back to the practice and assist my father."

"Yes, that's probably for the best. Do you want me to escort you back to Harley Street?"

She smiled at him. "I think I can find my way back there. I managed to get from Holland Park to there."

"Holland Park?"

"I'm staying with my father for the time being, just until I find my own place, but I have to say that I'm enjoying his town house in Holland Park. It's peaceful there. So different from Glasgow."

"Yes, Holland Park is one of my favorite places. I have a flat in Notting Hill, actually. I have a very spacious flat."

"You're not far away, then," she said.

Thomas shrugged. "As you said, Harley Street is not far from Kensington. Twenty some odd minutes on Westway."

"As long as it's not jammed." They chuckled together

over that goofy private joke. A blush tinged her cheeks and she tucked an errant strand of brown hair behind her ear, drawing his attention to her long slender neck. It was in that moment that pink tinged her creamy white skin that he knew he was in serious trouble. She was beautiful.

He had to make his excuses and get out of there. It was best if he kept his distance from her. They were business partners and nothing more. That's all they could be and the fact that he had to keep reminding himself of that was not a good sign.

"Well, I have some other surgical patients to make rounds on. I'll leave you to your work." It was a complete lie. There was no one else to see, but the more he lingered here the harder it was to leave. He found himself enjoying her company.

"I'll see you later. I should head back to the practice." She nodded and walked away from him, doing what he couldn't do. And he watched her walk down the hall toward the elevators.

This was bad.

When had she gone from someone he loathed—someone he planned to put through her paces because he wanted Charles's practice all to himself—to not being able to tear himself away from her? Escorting her to the hospital and admiring the flush of her skin, the red of her lips and wondering what it would be like to take her in his arms and kiss her?

The moment you saw her.

Which was true. He may have been rude to her when she was in the doctors' lounge, but when he'd seen her sitting there, looking around, he couldn't help but be intrigued by her. Why she was there and who she was.

And he knew that he was in big trouble if he didn't tread carefully.

The problem was he wasn't sure if he could stop himself.

* * *

Why did I let my father make an appointment for me?

Geri tried to really listen to what the stylist was saying as she was wandered around Harvey Nichols, but all the dresses blurred together in a great amorphous blob of color. When she'd got back to Harley Street, she'd met some patients and then her father had announced that Jensen was taking her to Knightsbridge to buy a dress for the social gathering she didn't want to attend.

"As my heiress you have to attend."

"I'm not an heiress. I'm just a doctor from Glasgow."

"I'm sorry, Geraldine, but as my only child you are an heiress."

"Why couldn't I be illegitimate?"

"Believe me, your mother isn't the only one who regrets our marriage." Then he gasped. *"I didn't mean it like that. I didn't mean... I'm glad you're here, Geraldine."*

"I know, Father. It's okay."

Geri had chuckled over that. Her mother had often reminded her she'd made a mistake in marrying her father.

"I should've chose the other man. I would've been far better off. Of course, I wasn't keen on his child and told him so."

Her mother wasn't keen on children, period. Something Geri was painfully aware of. Still, she was her father's only child.

There weren't any other relatives either. There was no one but her. She was it and even though she didn't like it, she had to do her duty and mingle with the social elite in London.

She hadn't minded the ride to Knightsbridge. She'd been a bit tired after her long day, and had just not expected the stylist to pounce on her the moment she walked through the doors of the department store.

She'd even tried to fend her off by telling her she'd just

poke around the dresses on her own, but that was a definite faux pas.

Take a deep breath. It'll be over soon. All you have to do is pick one.

"Do you have anything in silver?" she asked. "I like silver."

The stylist gasped. "You need color! It's almost Christmas and this is a big event."

"It is?"

The stylist nodded. "Your father was quite insistent about you picking out something absolutely stunning."

"Yes, but the thing is I don't like to stand out too much."

Which was true.

To avoid her mother's ire she had always remained quiet and retreated into the background. She didn't like being the center of attention, because no good came from it. Then Frederick had spotted her in a crowd of interns and had singled her out.

It had been thrilling, but she hadn't earned his respect. Only disdain and censure when their relationship had ended. No other surgeon had trusted her.

There was no way she wanted to stand out at the Gileses' social event.

The stylist ignored her and was clucking away through the fabric about chiffon or some other such nonsense. Geri groaned and cursed inwardly and as she looked around the department store she caught sight of Mr. Ashwood across the floor.

He was with a young woman who was blonde, stunningly beautiful, lean and tall, but not as tall as him. She was clinging to his arm and they were laughing. A flash of jealousy coursed through her.

She shouldn't be surprised that Thomas had a beautiful significant other. He was incredibly handsome. Dark, intense and sexy as hell.

He was a bad boy wrapped up in a respectable package. *Stop it, Geri!*

He bent down and kissed the woman on the forehead. Geri looked away. She didn't want Thomas to recognize her.

"I think I've found the perfect dress for you!" the stylist announced as she took Geri's hand and pulled her toward the change rooms. "You'll love it."

"I'm sure I will." And hopefully by the time she'd tried on the dress and bought it, Thomas and his girlfriend would be gone.

Her father had paid for the dress and the stylist. So all Geri had to do was wait for it to be wrapped up. It was a lovely dress, but it was also the most expensive piece of clothing she'd ever owned. Usually she bought her clothes from fashionable, chic places that didn't cost an arm and leg.

She'd been a bridesmaid once at her friend's wedding just after medical school and that dress hadn't cost her what this dress was costing her father.

If the bridesmaid's dress hadn't been so hideous and teal, she would've just worn that to the social gathering.

She smiled secretly to herself. Maybe she should just return this designer gown and dig out that old teal monstrosity of lace and puffed sleeves to wear after all. Except she did really like the dress the stylist had picked out.

It was festive and Geri did so love Christmas.

When she walked out into the street she breathed in the fresh, crisp December air. It had just begun to snow softly and the Christmas lights were just starting to come on along Knightsbridge.

Jensen pulled up in her father's black town car. He got out and opened the door, but she wasn't quite ready to go back home to Holland Park just yet. She wanted to take a long leisurely walk and revel in Christmas.

It was her favorite time of the year, even if her mother wasn't a big celebrator of Christmas. Geri would spend her Christmases curled up on the couch, watching Christmas specials, and those happy families and stories of hope were the family love she'd secretly craved as a child.

Now this new life she found herself in felt overwhelming and she just wanted to take a moment and be by herself, soaking in the first real Christmas snow of December.

She handed Jensen the garment bag and a bag with various other accessories and shoes that went with it. "Can you take this home, Jensen? You can tell my father I've bought a dress and shoes. I'm going to go to his social function, but right now I just want to take a walk."

"Are you sure, my lady?"

"You don't need to call me that, Jensen."

He took the parcels. "I'm afraid I do."

"Then I'm sure. I'll be home later, but I'm thirty years old. I think I can manage a walk about town on my own."

He nodded. "Of course."

Jensen placed the items in the back of the car and drove away. Her father would be annoyed that once again she wasn't allowing Jensen to drive her home at night, but she didn't care. She needed a few moments to clear her mind.

Collect herself. She'd been unable to think straight when she'd been in the store. Actually, it had been a long time since she'd had the chance to really think straight, period. Finding her father and discovering who she was and being offered this partnership had been dizzying. She turned down a side street and wandered aimlessly while people bustled around her, doing their Christmas shopping. She was completely in her own thoughts when she ran smack dab into a muscular wall of a man.

"Whoa, are you quite…? Geraldine?"

Oh, no.

She glanced up to see Thomas Ashwood and his companion standing in front of her. They had just stepped out of a coffee shop and she hadn't been paying any attention and had run smack into the very person she wanted to avoid.

Curse Murphy.

"Mr. Ashwood, I'm surprised to see you here."

"I wouldn't think you would be too shocked as we were both in Harvey Nichols at the same time," he teased.

Heat bloomed in her cheeks as she realized he'd noticed she'd been there. "Were we?"

Thomas grinned. "We were."

Geri's glanced landed on the young woman next to Thomas, who was busy staring at her phone and looking completely bored. "Sorry for ruining your date."

The girl wrinkled her nose and laughed. "Date? Thomas is my elder half brother. And I do mean elder."

Thomas glared at her. "Yes, Zoe, that's quite enough out of you."

Zoe chuckled and then nodded at Geri. "It's a pleasure to meet you."

"Well, at least my half sister has manners." Thomas cleared his throat. "Dr. Geraldine Collins, I would like to introduce you to my half sister Zoe Western."

"I'm also illegitimate." Zoe grinned and Geri couldn't help but chuckle as Thomas rolled his eyes.

"Why do you feel the need to convey that to all my acquaintances?" Thomas groaned.

Zoe shrugged. "Usually they're a bit more shocked. She's not. Means she's worldly. I like that."

"Scamp, and what would you know about the world?" he asked.

Zoe playfully stuck out her tongue while Geri tried not to laugh.

"How much of an age difference is there between you two?" Geri asked.

"A lot," Zoe teased, while Thomas groaned. "I'm seventeen."

"Yes, but she's still not mature enough to take care of herself. Since our father died and her mother is working with Doctors Without Borders in Africa, I am currently Zoe's legal guardian." He smiled down at his younger sister with much tenderness. "We were just doing some Christmas shopping. She wanted to send her mother something nice to try to entice her back to London."

"Yes, so I can spend school holidays away from this tyrant," Zoe teased. "Which reminds me, a group of my friends are meeting over on Brompton Road at the cinema. Can I please go? Jennifer can give me a lift back to the flat."

"I suppose so, but I want you home by eleven."

Zoe rolled her eyes. "Yes, tyrant."

"Scamp." Thomas ruffled her hair.

"Nice to meet you, Dr. Collins." And with that Zoe left them, heading down Sloane Street back to Knightsbridge.

"I have to say I'm relieved she's your sister."

Thomas cocked an eyebrow. "Jealous, are we, Dr. Collins?"

"Hardly."

Liar.

"Then why are you so relieved?" he asked.

"Actually, I was worried that an older man was with a young girl. It looked a bit icky if you ask me."

Thomas laughed out loud. "Icky? Never heard that one before. And you do know many men in your father's circles have second or third wives who are scandalously younger than themselves. I mean, I saw Lord Twinsbury eyeing you up today. Perhaps you can be the next Lady Sainsbury?"

"No, thank you," Geri said. "Well, I won't keep you."

He grabbed her arm, stopping her from leaving. His

hand so strong on her arm, so reassuring it made her feel nervous, because it felt so good.

"You're not keeping me. Where are you off to?"

"I was just taking a leisurely stroll."

He cocked an eyebrow and then took her arm, slipping it through the crook of his arm. "In December at night?"

"Is there some sort of law against that?" she asked.

"No, but I'm thinking about the thousand fits your father is going to have."

"I'm thirty. He shouldn't worry so much."

"Maybe he's trying to make up for lost time?" Thomas suggested tentatively.

"It's hardly your place to say that, Mr. Ashwood," Geri replied icily. But a niggling voice in her head had said the same thing.

"True. Just a suggestion. From one gentleman regarding another gentleman.

Geri smiled. "Yes, you are a gentleman, aren't you? I don't know of another man who would take time out of his night to walk a new business partner down some random street in the snow."

"You're obsessed with winter, it seems."

"No, just Christmas."

"I don't get Christmas."

"What don't you get about Christmas?"

He shrugged. "It was never a big deal when I was growing up. I mean, I guess I didn't have a loving family. Detached was more like it. So Christmas was just another day."

"Same here," she said. "But I loved the idea of it being something more. Which made me just want to love it all the more the older I got."

"Well, it did get considerably better when Zoe came on the scene. It was nice being able to buy toys and dolls when I was young man and celebrating Christmas with her and her mother."

"Were they together long, Zoe's mother and your father?"

Thomas shrugged. "Long enough. But Zoe's mother wouldn't marry my father. She was smart."

"Why?"

"He was… He had a lot of resentment. He never did get over my mother's death."

"I'm sorry."

Thomas shrugged. "Zoe's mother always made me feel like a son. Didn't have much of a mother figure growing up and my father was distant. I lost my mother when I was very young. I don't recall her, but people have told me my father was happy. Though I never saw it."

"I understand. My mother was not the most pleasant. I'm sorry about your mother."

He nodded. "Yes, I was heartbroken. It was a myo-cardial infarction during a pregnancy that did it. The baby died as well. She wasn't far along when it happened. Crushed my father. He didn't really get over her."

Geri squeezed his arm. "That's nice they loved each other. My parents did *not* love each other. They were two ships that passed in the night."

"You sure about that?" he questioned.

"Of course. Why wouldn't I be?"

"They married."

"So?" Geri shrugged. "Love and marriage don't always go hand in hand."

"Still, there must have been some feelings."

"Whatever feelings they had I don't wish to discuss." She shuddered. "Why are you so adamant they were in love?"

He shrugged. "I heard different."

Geri pulled him to a stop and to one side so they

wouldn't get trampled by the Christmas shoppers on the sidewalk. "What do you know?"

"Nothing, just rumors."

"Tell me."

He opened his mouth to say something but his pager went off, as did hers. Thomas reached his first and pulled it out, frowning when he read the text.

"It's Lord Twinsbury. We have to get back to the hospital."

"I sent Jensen away," Geri fretted.

"Don't worry, my car is down the street." He grabbed her hand. "Let's go. Thankfully the hospital isn't far."

She nodded and let Thomas guide her along the busy road to his car. She still wanted to know what he knew about her parents, but right now Lord Twinsbury was the most important thing. Everything else could wait, because really what difference would it make if her parents had been in love thirty years ago?

It wouldn't change the past and wouldn't shape her future.

CHAPTER FOUR

"Suction, please." Thomas worked over Lord Twinsbury. The graft had thrown a clot and begun to leak. It was the first time in a long time Thomas had performed a coronary artery bypass graft that had failed, but it was one of those things that could happen. There were so many factors that could lead to the graft leaking.

He was annoyed, but as he worked on Lord Twinsbury he could see the tissue was friable and he had a hard time suturing. All he seemed to be doing was macerating the vessels and he couldn't take another one from the groin. He glanced up to see Geri watching from the viewing gallery.

She was biting her lip and pacing, which wasn't helping, but he understood. She was worried about their patient. Her first patient since she'd started working with her father. He had a sneaking suspicion she liked the old coot and, truth be told, he did too.

Come on.

There was a buzz from the gallery.

"Mr. Ashwood, may I suggest something?"

"I'm all ears, Dr. Collins." What she could possibly suggest he didn't know, but if he didn't get the graft to work, if he didn't get the vessels to connect, he would lose Lord Twinsbury and he refused to let the old man go.

"Does the hospital have any donated umbilical vessels

that can be used instead of trying to take another one from the patient?"

"Brilliant, Dr. Collins." He nodded to a surgical fellow who took off to see if that could be found while he continued to work on saving Lord Twinsbury's life. It didn't take long for the fellow to return with an umbilical vein, prepped, stripped and ready to go.

Thomas gently took and placed it just below the faulty graft, praying that this one would be stronger than the one before. He was impressed Geraldine had known to suggest it. It was a trick only a well-read surgeon would know.

"Take him off bypass." Thomas closed his eyes and waited with bated breath. He glanced up at Geri, who had her hands pressed against the glass, worrying her bottom lip as she watched too.

The bypass machine slowed, the whirring sound ending, and the blood was allowed to flow through the heart.

Come on.

He didn't have to wait too long before the heart began to beat on its own again. The new graft was holding and he sent up silent thanks. Geri was clapping and smiling in the gallery and he smiled to himself as he finished the operation.

It was the best part of his job, saving lives, and it reminded him he was healing hearts, so that others didn't have to go through the pain he and his father had gone through when his mother had died. So other families didn't have to be devastated.

He couldn't heal his own heart, but he'd made his peace with that. He wouldn't pass the fear he faced along to children. This would never be their life. After what had happened with his mother and father, he knew he couldn't trust himself to love that deeply, to put his own heart at risk. His existence for the last thirty-odd years had worked and that's how it would stay.

When he'd finished with Lord Twinsbury he left it to his cardiothoracic fellow to take their patient up to the ICU. Tonight he would have his fellow monitor Lord Twinsbury's vitals. Charles wouldn't be happy, but he was tired from pulling an all-nighter just recently and it was Zoe's first day back from boarding school for the Christmas holidays. He wanted to be there for her.

Even if she spent most of her free time with her friends.

At least he would be home for her.

He would be the constant for Zoe, which he'd never had as a child.

Thomas leaned over the sink in the scrub room, rolling his neck. Every part of him was hurting and he couldn't remember the last time he'd felt so bone weary.

"You did amazingly."

He turned to see Geri, in scrubs, standing just outside the scrub room.

"You changed into scrubs to come and tell me I'm amazing? I'm impressed."

Geri shrugged. "I was going to do rounds on a couple of patients of my father's who were admitted for minor issues, so I thought I would come down here and congratulate you on that nice save."

"I should've thought of umbilical veins. It was the farthest thing from my mind as I tried to make the anastomosis with the original vein graft work. Thank you for being my reason back there."

"It's part of my job." She blushed. "Thank you for the acknowledgment."

"You're welcome, but it's not part of your job. It's a surgeon's job," he said. "Why didn't you become a surgeon again?"

"I wanted to be in a clinic instead of an OR. I wasn't cut out to be a surgeon."

She'd said something similar before and he'd believed

her at the time, but now he didn't really believe her; she was being evasive. Something else had made her decide not become a surgeon.

"Are you staying tonight?" she asked, changing the subject.

"No, I want to be home and see if Zoe makes her curfew." He dried his hands. "I'll grab something vile from the cafeteria to eat and then head for my flat."

"Enjoy your vile dinner. I'm going to make my quick rounds and then head back to Holland Park. I'm sure my father is wondering why a dress and shoes made it home but I didn't."

"A dress?"

"Yes, for that social event I'm being forced to go to."

"Ah, I'd completely forgotten about it."

She snorted. "I don't blame you."

And though he shouldn't offer it, he couldn't help himself. "Well, if I'm still here when you've done your rounds I'll give you a ride home."

"Thomas, it's okay, really. You don't have to stick around. You've just done grueling surgery and you need to go home and check on your sister. Make sure she made her curfew."

"Of course."

She nodded. "I'll see you tomorrow at the office."

Thomas watched her walk away from the scrub room, her long delicate hands thrust deep into the pockets of her white lab coat. Her glorious hair was braided and piled under a hideous scrub cap, but she still looked very desirable.

And he hated himself for his weakness when it came to her.

It was well after midnight when the taxi pulled up in front of her father's Holland Park town house. The lights were still on and she had no doubt her father was pacing. It was sweet of him, but he needed his rest. Part of the reason for his retirement was because he had cancer. He was fighting it and he needed to conserve every last ounce of his energy.

It was bad enough he wasn't telling anyone besides her that he was fighting the disease. He even went so far as to go to another hospital on the far side of the city to get his treatment. That way no one would know.

He was stubborn.

Just like her. Or at least that's what her mother had always said. Something she'd clung to as a child when she'd been wondering who her father was.

She had resented him for taking so long to find her and even then only finding her when it was too late almost to form a proper relationship.

"You're here now, Geraldine. That's all that matters."

She paid her cabbie and pulled out her key. There was a thick blanket of snow on St. James's Gardens across the road from her father's townhome and the streetlights gave the snow a warm golden glow.

The steps up to the navy door of her father's home had been meticulously cleared. That had probably been Jensen, who had gone back to his own home, which was not far from her father's. Her father might be of the gentry, but, other than Jensen, Molly, the cleaning lady and cook, he didn't employ servants, whereas Geri knew that Lord Twinsbury did.

Of course, Lord Twinsbury lived in Hampshire and when he came to London stayed at his club.

She didn't even have a chance to get the key in the door when her father swung it open, frowning.

"Where were you?"

"I was at the hospital, doing rounds on two of your patients. I also stayed to make sure that Lord Twinsbury's repair surgery went off smoothly." She pushed past her father into the entranceway and took off her jacket, hanging it on a coat hanger.

"Repair surgery?" Her father asked, concerned. "What happened? Is Lionel okay?"

"The vein graft leaked. The anastomosis from the original coronary artery bypass graft wouldn't hold. His veins were very friable."

And she was glad she'd been in the gallery to suggest the alternative graft. It had been her first surgical triumph as a resident on her first solo coronary artery bypass graft. She'd used an umbilical vein to save a young woman's life when that young woman's veins had also been very friable.

It was her signature move.

Frederick had felt a bit threatened by her at that point. She was sure now it was that surgery that had destroyed their romance a year ago. Still, Lord Twinsbury's life had been saved, even if she hadn't been the one to do the surgery. Even though she hadn't been able to see the full surgery from the gallery, she'd closed her eyes and could see it all step by step in her mind while Thomas had operated. And as she'd watched from the gallery she'd realized how much she missed surgery. Painfully.

She missed holding a heart in her hand, because it was a beautiful thing indeed.

It was comforting and she loved its complexities.

"Blast," he cursed under his breath, shaking her from her thoughts. Her father then ran a hand through his white hair. "Do you want a drink?"

"It's midnight."

"Yes, I know, but I can't sleep anyway. Damn pain." Her father wandered into the sitting room and began to pour himself a drink. She could hear the crackle of a fire.

Geri sighed, sinking down onto the very comfortable couch. "Sure, I'll have a gin and tonic."

"I thought you were a whisky lass," her father teased, pouring her a small glass.

"Usually, but I do have to get up early and go to the hospital first to check on our patients. Do you start chemo tomorrow?"

"Yes." Her father sat down in his leather wing chair. "I do."

"I wish you'd just get treated at St. Thomas Aquinas. Who cares if people know you have cancer?"

"I care." Her father took a sip. "I want to keep it to myself. Private."

She understood his need for privacy. There were things about her life no one knew and didn't need to know. Like she was a disgraced surgical resident, for one thing.

"If you were at the hospital I could check on you."

Her father raised any eyebrow. "Would you, then?"

"Of course." And it was true. As angry as she was at him, she knew none of this was really his fault. He had told her when they'd met that her mother had purposefully obscured the knowledge of her existence, until he'd received a letter from her a month before they'd met, telling him that he had a daughter. Even then, she hadn't formally met her father until the results of the DNA test to prove that they were actually related had been available. Their first meeting in the laboratory after it was confirmed had been awkward, to say the least.

"She called you Geraldine."

"Yes. Your mother...my grandmother, I suppose, had that name?"

"Yes." Her father cleared his throat. "She did. It's my favorite name."

For so long she'd been mad at her father for not coming to find her, but when she'd met him she'd realized the damage and hurt her mother had caused for them both.

Which was another reason she lived with her father.

She wanted to get to know him better, but it was hard. It was hard to trust another parent.

They may be related by blood, but they were both strangers who had been hurt and loath to trust again.

"Geraldine, I don't want you to waste time on me. My oncologist at Meadowgate Hospital is one of the best. Jensen can stay with me. He's already offered, and didn't ask for a wage, though of course I will pay him. Damn fool."

Geri smiled. "Remind me to thank him later."

"He brought in your dress." Her father smiled. "You'll look stunning at the function this weekend."

"You looked?"

"Of course." He grinned. "You'll really turn heads at your unofficial debut."

She winced. "Don't remind me. I'm liable to make a bloody mess of it."

"There's the Scot I know and love." Her father chuckled and winked. Only he didn't know her and she had a hard time believing that he loved her. She wasn't even sure if she loved him. Cared for him, yes. He was a brilliant doctor, but love? That was going a bit too far for her. Besides, how did one love an absent parent? Or even a parent when she hadn't even got love from her mother. She didn't believe in love. Look what had happened with Frederick.

"I really would prefer not to go," she said, hoping he would take pity on her.

"It'll be good for you to go. You can meet eligible, respectable men."

"Are you trying to marry me off already?"

He shrugged. "You're a lady of means. You will attract attention, just make a wise choice."

"I don't need to get married. Doubt I ever will."

Because I always fall for the wrong guys.

Plus she couldn't risk her heart again. Frederick had destroyed every single piece of trust she'd had. Love just hurt and there was no room in her heart for it. The only thing she could rely on was medicine. That was her true love.

"Never say never." Her father winked and she groaned.

"I'm headed for bed. I suggest you are too." She set down the glass on the bar, putting an end to the conversation. This was not a Regency romance. She was not going to make a suitable match. If she ever did decide to get married she was going to do so for love, not connections. She chuckled at that thought as she headed up the stairs to her room. She really doubted her father would go to bed any time soon.

She didn't blame him.

Cancer scared her as well.

She knew the reality of it. As did he.

And she wished it didn't have to be anyone's reality.

CHAPTER FIVE

"YOUR NEXT PATIENT is here to see you, Dr. Collins."

Geri looked up from her work. "Show them in, Ms. Smythe."

Mrs. Smythe nodded and disappeared. Geri was rather enjoying her time in the office. She liked getting to know her new patients. And sitting down to do reports was better than charting while standing up at a nurses' station, but it was the silence in between patients that she found a bit hard. The hustle and bustle of a hospital was far more relaxing to her than the quiet. It was getting to her.

The door opened wider and she was shocked to see Thomas's little sister Zoe enter her office. And she looked extremely nervous. She could tell by the way her green eyes were shifting around the office and she wouldn't meet her gaze.

"Thank you, Ms. Smythe," Geri said, dismissing the receptionist.

When the door was shut Zoe took a seat in front of the desk. "Thank you for seeing me."

"You wanted to see me?" Geri asked, and then she started worrying about all the reasons a seventeen-year-old girl might need to see a doctor she was familiar with.

Zoe nodded. "I chose a day that I knew my brother

wouldn't be here. Your father has been seeing me every time I come home."

Oh. No.

Her mind immediately jumped to the obvious, but then it dawned on her that she'd said she was seeing Charles as a doctor. So it couldn't be that.

She was confused and checked the computer for Zoe Western. "He doesn't have a file on you."

Zoe reached into her bag and handed her a file. "Your father let me keep it because of patient confidentiality and I don't want my brother knowing."

She took the file from Zoe and flipped it open, scanning the pages. "You have an atrial septal defect?"

Zoe nodded. "I was born with it and it went away, but when I was ten the hole opened up again. My mother took me to see your father and he referred me to a surgeon who did the catheterization. Thomas was at school then."

"It didn't work, though? You have a pacemaker?" Geri asked, as she flipped through eight years of medical reports.

"An arrhythmia. Your father has been caring for me since I was ten and I'm hoping you can do the same, under the condition that my brother doesn't know."

Geri shut the folder. "Why don't you want your brother to know?"

"Did he tell you his mother died of a heart attack?" Zoe asked, hedging because it was apparently a sensitive subject.

"Yes. He did."

"When I was first born with the atrial septal defect I was hooked up to a machine to help me breathe. The doctors didn't know if I was going to live or not and…he almost ran off from school he was so worried. Then there was this huge fight with our father…"

Geri held up her hand. She didn't really want to hear this from Zoe. If Thomas wanted her to know, which she seriously doubted, he would tell her himself. Zoe did have a point, though—patient confidentiality—but she was under age.

"Thomas is your legal guardian. He should know."

"My mother is. Thomas is one of my guardians, but if you need to talk to someone you can contact my mother in Malawi."

She sighed. "Okay, I'll take you on."

"Thank you." Zoe grinned. "I'm so relieved. Your father was always so good to me and I knew you'd be as well."

"Because of my father?" Geri asked, confused.

"No, by the way Thomas was going on and on about you and your brilliant suggestion in the operating theater with Lord Twinsbury."

Geri blushed at the idea of Thomas praising her.

Don't think about it.

"So this is a regular visit?" she asked.

Zoe nodded. "Yes. I hope it is."

Geri got up. "You need a checkup on your pacemaker, by the looks of your file."

"Yes."

Zoe followed her into the exam room that was attached to her office and sat down on the exam table, taking off her top. Geri handed her a gown, giving Zoe some privacy while she got ready for the check.

She wheeled over her computer and Zoe lay down flat.

"You're an old pro at this," Geri teased.

Zoe laughed. "Just a bit."

"So I don't have to explain the procedure to you."

"You can if you want."

Geri grinned. "No, I think I'll pass."

"I'm ready."

She attached the electrodes to Zoe's chest and her legs and then pulled out the magnet, placing it over the pacemaker so the computer could read the pacemaker. Geri watched the reading and there was nothing to worry about. Zoe's pacemaker was working fine.

"Your father never mentioned you before," Zoe said. "Well, until last year."

"That's because he didn't know I existed until last year."

Zoe smiled. "Cool, we can form a club."

"Club?"

"Illegitimate debutantes."

Geri chuckled. "I hate to break it to you but my parents were married. They divorced after I was born. I'm not illegitimate."

"Oh," Zoe said with disappointment. "Well, you're no fun. I was hoping you were as well so we could both shock everyone."

"You're quite witty for a seventeen-year-old."

She shrugged. "You have met my brother, haven't you?"

"Very true." The computer finished its reading and Geri took off the electrodes and the magnet. "You're all done."

"Thank you, Dr. Collins, and I appreciate you helping me and not telling my brother."

"It was my pleasure, but, Zoe, I think you should tell him. I mean, it has to come from you."

"I know. Your father has said the same thing to me several times."

It warmed her heart to hear how her father cared for all his patients. Especially pediatric ones. A trait they shared.

"Well, your pacemaker is good to go for another year. You know the drill. If you have arrhythmias or any other strange symptoms, please go to the nearest hospital."

"I know." Zoe pulled on her shirt. "Why is your father retiring? I mean, it just came out of the blue."

"Well, he wants to travel more."

Zoe looked confused. "Really? I thought maybe his cancer had become worse."

"You know about his cancer?"

She nodded. "He told me. We talked a lot."

"Well, then, not travel." Geri shut off the computer. "My father's cancer is worse. Stage four stomach cancer."

Zoe's face fell. "I had a feeling it was something like that. I'm so sorry."

"He starts treatment today. He's in chemo. Across the city because, just like you and your secrecy about health concerns, he doesn't want anyone at his local hospital to know that he's suffering from cancer. He doesn't want any help at all beyond from his chauffeur."

Zoe chuckled. "Poor Jensen."

"Yes, but I don't think Jensen minds too much."

Zoe grabbed her coat and Geri handed her back her file. "Thank you, Dr. Collins. I'll see you around, I'm sure, and definitely next year for my next checkup."

"Yes."

Zoe left the exam room and Geri sighed as she wheeled the computer back to the corner of the room. She couldn't help but think about her father.

He didn't want her there, but maybe she should've forced him to have her there. Jensen was all well and good, but she was his daughter. Even if she didn't totally feel like his daughter yet, she was still that.

She had a sense of duty.

The door in the exam room opened and Thomas peeked in. "Sorry, was that my sister Zoe that I saw leaving here?"

Blast.

"Yes, it was. She was looking for you and you weren't here. You just missed her. She's on the way to do some shopping with some friends." Geri worried her lip and hope that her lie went over with Thomas.

She wasn't the best liar ever and for one moment she saw a flicker of disbelief in Thomas's eyes.

"Oh, well, sorry I missed her. I got tied up with a cauterization and, of course, checking on Lionel." He grinned sardonically.

"I didn't think you were allowed to use his name?" Geri teased.

"I know, but he'll never know, now, will he?" Thomas tapped the side of his nose. "So what are you doing for the rest of the day? I know you don't have any more patients."

She cocked an eyebrow. "How do you know that?"

"I checked with Ms. Smythe."

"Why would you do that?" she asked cautiously, afraid of what his motives were, and then she cursed herself for questioning his motives. When had she become so untrusting?

"I was wondering if you wanted to have a ride over to the hospital where your father is getting his chemotherapy."

"How…how did you know?"

"I have a friend who works in Oncology at Meadowgate Hospital and he mentioned Dr. Collins had checked in. He thought I knew when he accidentally broke confidentiality."

"My father is not going to be happy that you know. He wanted it to be kept secret."

"I won't say a word. My lips are sealed. So, do you want to go?"

Yes. No.

"He didn't want me there. I think I'll honor his wishes. I don't think he'd be particularly happy if he found out that you'd brought me, as well."

"Ah, point taken."

Geri moved out to her office and Thomas followed her.

"Don't you have patients to see?"

Thomas glanced at his wrist. "Not for another two hours. Do you want to get some lunch?"

"No." She laughed. Why was he so persistent? Couldn't he take a hint?

"What's so funny?"

"Are you the only surgeon who has such an open schedule? You're so different from the surgeons I knew in Glasgow. They never even had time to have a coffee."

"I serve a very different clientele here than the surgeons in Glasgow, I'm sure."

"I'm sure, Lord Hoity-Toity."

Thomas laughed. "I'm not exclusive to the 'hoity-toity,' as you put it. Anyone who wants my service, if I get the proper referral, can come and see me. Not all the hoity or toity come, though."

"Don't they?" she teased.

He rolled his eyes. "Okay, some do. I am the best."

She rolled her eyes. "I have a lot of work to do."

"Fine, then just turn down the best new café around here and a chance to have lunch with me."

"I'm sure I'll survive." Her phone buzzed and she saw a text from Jensen.

Your father has collapsed. He's not well. Please come.

"What's wrong?" Thomas asked.

"My father. I have to get to Meadowgate Hospital. He's collapsed."

"Come on, I'll take you."

"And what about your patients this afternoon?"

"I'll drop you off. I don't want to upset your father."

Geri nodded and grabbed her coat. Why did Thomas have to be so good to her? He barely knew her, but he'd gone from the standoffish jerk of their first meeting to her first real friend in London.

She didn't deserve that, given that she was rarely, if ever, friendly to him, but right now she'd take it.

Thomas had finished seeing his last patient and the support staff had gone home, but he lingered at the office, hoping that Geraldine would return. Which was foolish, but Geraldine was dedicated to her work. She seemed to retreat into her work a lot.

Of course, he did exactly the same thing.

And as if on cue, he heard the key at the front door of their practice and the security code entered.

"Shouldn't you be home, taking care of your father?" He asked.

Geraldine let out a small scream. "My God, man, you scared me."

Thomas chuckled to himself, hearing the Scottish burr slip out. "Sorry, I didn't mean to scare you."

"And what're you doing here? Shouldn't you be at home?" she asked accusingly, her voice still shaking. The accent was still there and fires of rage burned in her hazel eyes.

"No, no, you need to answer my question first."

Geraldine sighed and peeled off her coat, hanging it up. "I need to finish a couple of my charts. My father is stable and is now an inpatient at Meadowgate. He had a bad reaction to the chemotherapy. He'll be there for a couple of days."

"I'm sorry to hear that." And he was truly sorry. He liked Charles.

She shrugged. "Chemotherapy is hard. So now I've answered your question you can answer mine. Quid pro quo, my friend. Why are you still here?"

"I had some charting to catch up on as well. Surgical reports to send off to general practitioners who referred their patients to me. As well as one for you. I've emailed it to you."

"Really?"

"Of course. Lord Twinsbury. Is he not your patient? I do his surgical procedures, but you're his cardiologist. I've also sent one to his general practitioner."

"You're on the ball."

He shrugged. "I like to get loose ends tied up before the Christmas holiday."

"I thought you weren't a fan of Christmas?" she said.

"Ah, but Zoe is and I don't want her to be alone, with me working endless rounds at the hospital and doing surgeries to get through the holiday. Like I used to do."

She smiled at him, a warm smile that made his heart skip a beat. She rarely bestowed them, it seemed. "Very admirable of you."

"I'm going to order in some dinner, continue working. Would you like me to order something for you?"

She seemed to hesitate but then relaxed. "What're you ordering in?"

"That French café also does deliveries."

"Oh, I would love some French food. Surprise me."

He grinned. "Are you sure about that?"

"Nothing weird like brains. I don't mind snails, but I draw the line at brains."

"Fair enough."

She headed into her office and Thomas went to his to place the order. He ordered a variety of the café's most delectable dishes, all of which could be served with the Cabernet Sauvignon he had in his office.

When the food came, he grabbed the bottle of wine and two glasses and knocked on her office door.

"Your food, my lady."

Geraldine looked up. "It smells very good."

"It is good, I assure you." He set down the take-away

bags after she cleared her desk and then the bottle of wine and the two glasses. She cocked an eyebrow in question, seeing the two wineglasses.

"I don't know many surgeons who keep wine and wine glasses in their office."

"Don't you?" he teased as he popped the cork and poured out the wine. "I always have wine on hand to seduce women after hours."

Geraldine laughed. "Oh, really? And who would you be seducing after hours?"

"Doris, the cleaning lady." He waggled his eyebrows and she laughed as he set out the aluminum containers and plastic utensils. "Sorry, my level of sophistication ends with the wineglasses."

"It's okay. It all smells so wonderful I'm ready to eat it with my hands."

"You should laugh more, instead of showing the austere, reserved facade you're trying to pass off to everyone. It suits you."

A blush crept up her cheeks. "I laugh when something is funny. I'm not a total ice queen."

"People at St. Thomas Aquinas beg to differ on that point."

She groaned. "It's just better to keep things professional."

"Oh, well, I can take the food away..." he teased.

"Don't you dare."

He poured the wine. "Can you guess what I've ordered?"

"Since you're serving a Sauvignon I'm going to assume garlic. That, and I can smell it."

"Yes, Coquilles St. Jacques, *aligot*, crusty bread and madeleines are the menu tonight."

"*Aligot* is a word I'm not familiar with." She leaned over. "Smells good, though."

Thomas pulled it out and opened it. "Mashed potatoes

with garlic and melted cheese essentially. *Aligot* sounds much more sophisticated."

Geraldine took a paper plate and he served her a bit of everything and then dished up his own, sitting across from her. He raised his glass. "To a new partnership."

"Cheers," she said, clinking her glass against his. "I have to say this is the nicest and most delicious work dinner I've ever had. I thought grabbing a pot noodle on rounds was as good as it got."

Thomas wrinkled his nose. "Travesty. Though it usually is. This is a rarity."

She smiled and his blood heated. He liked it when she smiled at him and he couldn't help but wonder what it would be like to kiss those lips, to feel her pulse race under his fingertips and wrap her up in his arms, bringing her to ecstasy.

Whatever he had, he had it badly for Geraldine. Usually, with any other woman, he would pursue her, and date her for a short time, until they realized that he was completely dedicated to his work and they would drop him. As soon as they realized he had no intention of settling down, the brief affair would be over and he wouldn't look back.

That's what living with hypertrophic myocardiopathy afforded him. The devastation his father had carried when his mother had died was something he would never wish on anyone. He'd taken a leap of faith when he'd had a fling with Cassandra, but then she'd broken it off and he'd taken it as a sign.

He was meant to be alone. It was better that way.

Only he couldn't do that with Geraldine. She was his partner, the daughter of a man he admired. There was no way he could seduce her to purge her from his system. So why was he bothering with this silly pursuit? The best idea would be to put distance between them but, try as he may, he gravitated to her.

He was drawn to her. He hadn't realized how lonely he was.

"This is heavenly," she said between mouthfuls. "Good choice."

"Thank you," he said. "I spent some time in France in my youth so I'm a bit of a connoisseur."

"I've never been to France. I would love to go to Paris one day."

"I'm sure you'll go one day. I mean you have the money now," he teased.

"I don't. My father does."

"You're his heiress, are you not?"

She frowned, her face unreadable. "Yes, and what of it?"

"Don't get defensive. I'm not a fortune hunter. I'm just stating a fact that as an heiress who stands to inherit a pretty penny you'll be able to afford to go to Paris one day."

"True, but Paris is the city of romance, is it not? I don't want to go there alone."

"Why not? I think it can be a great place to be alone. To get lost in yourself."

She cocked her head to one side. "Is that what you did?"

"Once or twice. I love France, as well."

She was staring at him with a dreamy expression, one he knew all too well from his past conquests. This was heading in the wrong direction fast. He needed to change the subject.

"So what was your mother like?"

"Unpleasant." Geraldine frowned. "She had moments of tenderness, but really I don't think she cared for me."

"Makes you wonder why she kept you and didn't hand you over to Charles."

Geraldine nodded. "I've thought about that too. I guess she just didn't want to make anyone happy. She didn't get along with her parents, she didn't have many friends. Men friends, yes."

"You do know that my father was the other man."

She almost choked. "What?"

He grinned. "Unfortunately, I was the boy who drove your mother into your father's arms. Enraged my father something fierce. It's why your father and my father hated each other. They were both vying for the same woman."

"Be thankful your father didn't marry my mother. It would've been terrible."

"From what you say, I gather that, but honestly how much worse could she have made it? I was already pretty miserable."

"I'm sorry, Thomas." And she smiled at him warmly.

I'm sorry too. They came from different worlds, but really they were the same.

You need to put some distance between you.

He took that warning to heart and stood up.

"Well," he said, clearing his throat and cleaning up the empty containers, "I have a long day of surgery ahead of me tomorrow. I'll get this mess out of your way so you can get back to work and I'll head back to my flat."

A blush tinged her cheeks and she swept an errant strand of hair behind her ear. "Of course, yes. I have a lot of charting to finish up. I don't want to be here all night."

Thomas nodded. "Good night, Geraldine."

"'Night, Thomas."

He left her office, shutting the door behind him. He lingered briefly in the hall then headed back to his office. There was no way he could purge her from his system. He couldn't pursue a friendship or anything more with Geraldine. Things had to be completely professional.

Or he'd forget himself completely and put his heart at risk.

CHAPTER SIX

GERI WAS PACING and still trying to figure out a way to get out of going. Social functions had never been her forte in the past. She was a bit of a wallflower and the couple of times she'd accompanied Frederick somewhere she'd felt very out of place and unwelcome. And she had a sneaking suspicion that she would be unwelcome at this function as well. She was, after all, Lord Collins's estranged daughter.

"You're worrying for nothing, Geraldine."

She glanced up the stairs. Her father was standing at the mirror on the landing, adjusting his bow tie.

"And how do you know I'm worried?" she asked.

"Easy. You pace, just like me."

Geri smiled and then went up the few steps to the landing to help her father with his bow tie.

"You're hopeless at this. I thought a lord would know better," she teased.

"I have someone dress me usually." He was teasing her back and it was nice. Usually he was so careful, so polite.

"There," she said, smoothing his lapels. "All done. What would you do without me?" Then she blushed when she realized what she'd said and she could see the sadness in her father's eyes. A brief flicker of regret.

And she shared it, as well.

All those wasted years her mother had stolen from them.

She cleared her throat.

"You really shouldn't be going to this social event, Father. You've only been out of the hospital for three days."

Her father walked down the stairs slowly. "Nonsense, you're just trying to get out of it."

"I'm not."

Liar.

She was totally trying to get out of it. At least she didn't have to go to the horse show. She liked horses, she just wasn't really *into* them all that much, and enclosed stadiums full of animals were not her thing.

"You look stunning, by the way," her father said as he adjusted the cuff links on his tuxedo. "Absolutely stunning."

She was pleased by that. The dress was bronze-colored, with a fitted strapless bodice and a full taffeta skirt that was bustled up in a haphazard way. She felt very awkward in it, but she'd always secretly dreamed of wearing a dress like this, though after a certain point she'd stopped dreaming about it because she'd thought it would never happen.

Even at school formals, her mother had got her dresses from charity shops because her mother didn't believe in feeding the consumeristic fashion industry.

Vintage was better.

Only Geri secretly craved fashion and being chic.

That was the only upside to this social function, because she was absolutely dreading everything else. She didn't know anyone there and certainly didn't know how to talk to them. She knew nothing about the International Horse Show.

Once she got there and her father was satisfied that she'd met enough people, she'd retreat to a corner and try to stay unnoticed until her father grew tired enough that he'd leave. And she was sure that, given his bad reaction to the chemotherapy, their jaunt out tonight to this ball would not be long.

Her father was having a hard time coming down a flight of stairs. She doubted he would be able to do much socializing tonight. She wrapped her wrap around her shoulders so she wouldn't freeze in the December weather.

"Shall we?" He held out his arm, smiling at her.

"Of course. Let's get this over with."

"Geraldine, don't be such a Debbie Downer. You'll have fun. Who knows, you might meet an eligible and suitable young man."

"So you keep saying, but I'm not looking. Right now it's my career, as I've told you before."

"I can live in hope."

"You're a romantic? You?"

Her father nodded. "Yes. In spite of the hand love dealt me, I'm still hopeful."

She squeezed his arm. She wished she had his optimism, but when love had dealt her a bad hand she'd known it was better to cut her losses than remain hopeful.

Marriage was not in the cards for her.

Jensen was waiting at the bottom of the stairs for them. He held open the door and Geri slid in first, tucking her skirt as her father climbed in beside her. There was a pained expression on his face. He winced as he shifted.

"Are you sure you should be going tonight?" she asked again.

"Positive," he snapped. "I'm fine, Geraldine. I've never missed this event and I'm damned if I'll miss it now."

She shook her head. "You'll regret it in the morning."

"I can live with that."

They stopped arguing when Jensen got into the car. They rode in silence to Mayfair, where the Gileses were holding the ball. The street and the drive were jam-packed with luxury cars and limousines.

"I'm sure their neighbors love them," Geri mumbled at the congestion.

"Most of the neighbors are invited." Her father smiled at her and took her hand. "Relax. It'll be fine."

Jensen pulled up and parked. He opened the door and her father got out first, then helped her out. Geri tried not to shake with nervousness as her father led her up to the front door.

She was stunned by the beauty of the home and by all the people dressed to the nines. There was a huge Christmas tree at least fifteen feet tall in the foyer. It was decorated in traditional Victorian ornaments and candles.

It was like nothing she'd ever seen before. It was like something from a magazine.

"You've stopped shaking," her father teased.

"It's beautiful," she whispered.

"Admit it. You're glad you came."

"Only a bit." She smiled at her father and gave him a little side hug. "I do like Christmas trees."

Her father just grinned at her and led her down the stairs through the foyer. Above the tree was a large chandelier, which accentuated the large spiral staircase.

"Are you quite all right?" Her father asked as he handed her a flute of champagne.

"I think so." She took the flute and laughed. "Still nervous, but this is just wonderful."

Her father nodded. "I'm going to say hello to our host and hostess. Will you be okay if I leave you for a moment?"

"Of course." Geraldine had already met the host and hostess and her father knew she was nervous about this event enough to make pleasantries.

She walked slowly around the tree, admiring the decorations and listening to the chatter around. There was a group of woman about her age. Debutantes. They barely spared her a glance, but she didn't care. She just stood there, admiring all the Christmas decorations and taking in the sights of a beautiful London home decked out for Christmas.

"I can't believe they invited Duke Weatherstone and that he actually came. He never comes to these things." The ladies began to chatter loudly.

"I heard that he actually seduced Harriet Poncenby, but since he didn't want to get married ever, she dropped him."

"He's devilishly handsome, though."

Geri chuckled to herself as she listened to the gossip and she couldn't help but wonder who this Duke Weatherstone was because she'd heard so much about him. All she could imagine was a middle-aged Lothario, because even though these socialites thought he was devilishly handsome, she doubted very much that he would live up to expectations.

No one ever did.

"He did, he actually came to this event and he looks so handsome in that tuxedo. Too bad he brought his half sister with him."

Geri whipped around to see who they were talking about and she gasped when she saw that it was Thomas and Zoe who were coming down the stairs.

Thomas? He's the Duke of Weatherstone.

And the women were right, he was devilishly handsome in that designer tuxedo. His dark hair was perfectly groomed and a mischievous, devil-may-care smile flitted about his lips. It made her feel weak in the knees and her pulse race. She'd been attracted to Thomas before, he was very handsome, but seeing him like this made her swoon just a bit.

Zoe looked gorgeous in a dark green velvet dress that accentuated her blond hair, the complete opposite of her dark brother. She also looked uncomfortable, but then her gaze met Geri's and she waved. Geri waved back, stunned.

Thomas turned and looked at her and that smile disappeared, replaced by an expression she couldn't read.

Warmth spread across her cheeks and she knew she was blushing.

Run.

He was heading toward her and there was no escaping now.

Zoe moved away to a group of friends who were waving her over, so by the time Thomas reached her it was just the two of them, but she was sure everyone was staring at them as they stood beside that big tree.

"You look beautiful," Thomas said. He took her hand in his and bent over it, kissing the knuckles. His hot breath fanning against her skin made a shiver of anticipation run down her spine. "Just absolutely stunning."

"Thank you," she whispered, finding her voice again.

"I do believe I've rendered you speechless." He grinned. "Good."

"Good?"

"All right, not exactly good, but I quite like being able to take your breath away."

"Thomas, or should I say the Duke of Weatherstone. You're a duke? So when were you planning to inform me? I am, after all, your business partner. Shouldn't I know these things?"

"That's a lot of questions."

"Well, I'm a bit shocked you're a duke."

"Yes, I'm afraid so." He winked.

"The Dark Duke, that's what they call you? Seducer of debutantes."

"And where did you hear that?" He asked.

"It's the *on dit* here tonight." Geri nodded slightly in the direction of the group of ladies, who sent her pointed stares.

He winced. "Again, guilty."

"I don't think I should be associating with you, Your Grace. You're liable to ruin my reputation," she teased, letting her guard down just slightly because she was enjoying her conversation with him.

Dangerous move.

He was a seducer. This was his game and she suddenly felt like the prey, only she wasn't sure she minded too much at the moment.

There was a twinkle in his eyes as he smiled. "Since when did you care about reputation?"

She froze, worrying that he knew something about Glasgow, about Frederick. "I don't... I don't care about reputation."

"Don't get missish on me. I'm only teasing."

She couldn't help but laugh in relief. "You look very svelte," she said, changing the subject.

"Why, thank you. I am, after all, in the line of succession." He ran a hand over his lapels. "I have to look somewhat dashing. I do have a reputation to uphold since I'm a dark seducer of innocents."

"You're such a rogue."

"I'll take that as a compliment."

And then before she could help herself the words tumbled from her lips. "You should. I have a soft spot for rogues."

Thomas cocked an eyebrow, but his pulse began to race the moment Geri said she had a soft spot for rogues. There was a slight twinkle in her eyes and if she'd been anyone else, he might have taken her up on that.

Except she was completely off-limits. He wouldn't seduce Charles's daughter.

Blast.

He'd known she was going to be here and he'd planned to stay away from the event, because he'd managed to stay away from her the last few days. Zoe had been very insistent on coming because of her friends who were planning to attend.

So he'd steeled his resolve and planned to hide away in the corner, but then she'd been standing there beside the tree, looking breathtakingly beautiful in that gown, her hair swept up, her back bare so he could admire the graceful sweep of her long neck.

Then she looked at him and he was lost and for a moment he forgot why he was staying away from her.

She's your colleague. Not a conquest.

"Is your father here?" he asked, trying to change the subject.

"Yes. He went over to speak to the host and hostess." She nodded in that direction and he saw Charles smiling and laughing, though he looked terrible. Charles's face was so gaunt.

"The chemotherapy is hard on him, I can see." Thomas sighed. "It's a shame."

Geraldine frowned. "Yes. I told him we should just stay home, but he was insistent on coming and was very insistent on me attending.'

"Of course. This is your first formal function as his daughter."

"Why didn't you tell me you were a duke?" she asked again.

Thomas shrugged. "It's not something I like to brag about. It's just a title. I'm a surgeon. That I will brag about."

"I don't blame you for that in the least." Then she laughed. "A duke living in a flat in Notting Hill."

"I may have stretched the truth a tad. I'm afraid I live in quite a large house in Notting Hill. Staff quarters, the whole thing."

"A flat is what you said."

Thomas shrugged. "Well, my room is like a flat."

Geraldine rolled her eyes and music began to filter out of the ballroom. Even though he shouldn't, he decided he couldn't resist taking her in his arms, even just for tonight, and having a dance. He took her half-filled champagne flute and set it down. Then he took her hand.

"What're you doing?" she asked.

"We're going to have a dance."

"No, I don't think that's wise," she said, dragging her feet.

"I think it's very wise. Besides, what harm can it do? We're friends, right?"

"No," she said. "We barely know each other."

"Well, coworkers, then. Come on."

"I'm a terrible dancer," she said.

"I'll lead. It's not a problem." He winked at her and gave a tug and she followed after him into the ballroom where people were dancing to the slow music played by the live band. He spun her round and then pulled her flush against him, before leading her out on the dance floor. His hand was on the small of her back as he led the dance.

"You know how to dance?"

"Of course. I'm a duke." He winked at her and she laughed at his joke but turned her head away.

It felt so good, having her in his arms. He was cursing himself inwardly for doing something so unlike him again. He was pursuing the wrong woman. He couldn't have her. Only as they moved across the dance floor in sync, his resolve was weakening, because he did want her.

She was forbidden fruit and he was sorely tempted. Geraldine deserved a man who could give her everything he couldn't. He had money to support her, but he didn't have a heart to give her. He couldn't give her a family, even though that's what he wanted to do.

Geraldine had been through enough pain. Just like him. She deserved more.

"Come on, this dance can't be all that bad, Geraldine."

A pink blush tinged her cheeks. "No, it's not. It's actually my first dance. I was a bit of a wallflower growing up. No one ever asked me to dance."

"No one? They were out of their minds then. You're a fantastic dancer, for the most part because that was my toe you just stepped on."

"Sorry," she said. Then she laughed. "Although you do deserve it for forcing me out here."

He shrugged. "It's quite all right."

"Your sister looks beautiful tonight." Geraldine nodded in the direction of Zoe standing on the edge of the dance floor smiling at him as they moved past.

"Yes, she's a brat of the highest order. She's the one who forced me out here tonight."

"And what does she think of her brother being the notorious Dark Duke?"

He grinned. "She thinks it's funny, if a bit disturbing. She adores me, though, so it doesn't matter what I do as long as I'm up-front with her. We don't hide anything from each other."

A strange expression passed over her face.

"What?" he asked.

"Nothing. Just envious of your sibling relationship. I was an only child." Geraldine smiled. "Zoe is a wonderful young woman. You should be proud."

"I am." He glanced back at his sister. "She's my pride."

And the closest thing he'd have to having a daughter.

The dancing ended and they stood there for a moment at the edge of the dance floor while the other dancers clapped the band. He still held onto her, staring down into those deep green eyes. He was so close he could reach down and just kiss her.

"Come on," he whispered in her ear, drinking in her perfume.

"Where are we going?"

"I'm going to give you a reputation worthy of a lady." He winked at her.

She blushed, but followed him to a curtained alcove by a window. It was dark in there and she was trembling in his arms.

"Thomas," she whispered. "This isn't wise."

"I'm not going to do anything." Though he wanted to. "You should've seen everyone looking at you. Looking at us. I have to keep up the appearance of being something of a rogue, so I can get all those matchmaking mothers off my back. I'm a highly desirable bachelor."

"I guess, with your pedigree, you would be highly desirable." She sighed. "My father is pushing me to find a suitable match. Like I need to be married."

Thomas was intrigued. "You don't want to get married?"

"No. Not particularly."

"Why?"

"Does it matter? Why do I have to get married?"

"So, you wouldn't be against a bit of romance that didn't end in something more?"

Don't. You can't have her. Charles's daughter.

"No, I wouldn't mind," she whispered. "I don't need any promises made to me."

His pulse thundered in his ears and he reached down to touch her cheek, which looked almost like alabaster in the moonlight filtering through the window. She didn't need marriage, didn't want it. Just like he didn't want it. Perhaps he could just indulge once. Just one kiss. He was going to lean down and kiss her, but at that moment a scream rent the air.

They came out of the curtained alcove and looked back toward the dance floor to see what the commotion was about. Geraldine saw it first.

"Zoe!" Geraldine shouted, picking up her skirts and running.

Thomas spun around in time to see his sister crumple to the floor and go into a seizure before her body went rigid. By the time he got to her, she wasn't breathing.

"Call emergency services and get a defibrillator here immediately," he screamed above the din. He was handed one and charged it and was about to place the pads on her chest.

"No, you can't!" Geraldine yelled, throwing herself over Zoe's body.

"What're you doing?" Thomas shouted.

"Zoe has a pacemaker. If you shock her with incorrect placement of the paddles, she'll die."

CHAPTER SEVEN

"PACEMAKER?" THOMAS SAID, dumbfounded, as Geraldine did chest compressions. He was angry at himself for not acting faster. For not knowing about Zoe's pacemaker. For hesitating.

Wake up!

"Yes," she answered. "They need to be an inch away if you're going to shock her."

"I know," Thomas snapped. He adjusted the pads an inch away from where Geraldine indicated the device was implanted. "Clear."

Geraldine moved her hands and he shocked his baby sister. It almost too much to bear, watching her convulse as the electric shock moved through her, trying to start her heart again. It was more than he could bear and he cried out as he watched her. The only real family he had. The only one who'd loved him unconditionally since his mother.

"Let me do that," Charles said gently, taking the paddles from his hands. "You can't, you're family."

Thomas mumbled his thanks and took a step back. Feeling lost and helpless, all he could do was watch. It was agonizing.

Geraldine continued chest compressions. "I think the pacemaker stopped firing."

"When was the last time she had it checked?" Thomas demanded.

"Three days ago. She came to see me, and it was fine," Geraldine said.

Thomas was so angry. Why hadn't anyone told him that Zoe had a pacemaker, and since when? He also wanted to know who had put it in. He was ready to throttle whoever had. He felt like his trust had been violated, and he felt like a complete fool for saying that Zoe and he never hid anything from each other.

She clearly did and for one moment he wasn't sure if he could trust anyone.

No wonder Geraldine had looked so oddly at him, it was because she knew the truth. She knew there was something that Zoe had been hiding from him. He felt betrayed and hurt. There was no one he could trust.

"Clear," Charles shouted.

Geraldine stopped compressions and Thomas turned away, not wanting to watch has they shocked his sister again. This time, though, Zoe gasped for breath as the pacemaker obviously kicked back on.

Thank God.

"Zoe, you're okay," Geraldine whispered. "You're okay. Your pacemaker stopped working and you had a seizure."

Zoe didn't say anything, just nodded and took deep breaths. The paramedics arrived then and Thomas stood back as they loaded his sister onto a stretcher, Geraldine and Charles were telling the paramedics all the important health information.

Geraldine picked up her skirts and began to follow the paramedics out. Thomas raced after them and took Zoe's hand.

"I'm her brother and her guardian. I'm going with her," Thomas stated firmly, not letting his sister's hand go. He wouldn't leave her. He'd take care of her. He hadn't been able to save his mother all those years ago, but he'd save his little sister.

The paramedics nodded.

Zoe clung to her brother. She was shaking as she took deep breaths through the oxygen mask. Geraldine helped push the gurney out to the waiting ambulance. She climbed inside.

"You don't have to come, Geraldine. I have it from here." Thomas didn't want to take her from the party. Zoe was his responsibility. The truth was that he didn't want Geraldine to see him at this vulnerable moment with his sister. She couldn't see him like this. No one did. Only there was also a piece of him that wanted her there.

"I'm coming with you. I'm her doctor."

"No, you're not her doctor. I'm her doctor."

"No. You're her brother. You can't help and you know that. I am coming with you," Geraldine said firmly, but with tenderness that he appreciated.

Thomas nodded and then squeezed Geri's hand in thanks. She was right. He had no choice. He was Zoe's brother, family, and there was no way he could be her doctor right now because doctors couldn't work on their own family members. He had to let Geraldine help him.

"What if she needs surgery? You can't help her then," Thomas said. "I'm the cardiothoracic surgeon."

"No, but I can find someone who can. We'll get her help, don't worry." She squeezed his hand back, her touch reassuring. It felt so good to have that human connection. No one had ever shown him compassion like this before. He didn't know what he'd been missing.

Thomas didn't say anything further.

Still, he felt angry and hurt he hadn't known about Zoe's pacemaker. How could both Charles and Geraldine hide this from him? They were his partners. How could Zoe hide this from him? He felt hurt and he felt betrayed, but there was nothing he could do right now.

Right now his focus had to be on his little sister. And he was angry at himself for not seeing the signs of her condition. He was a cardiothoracic surgeon, for God's sake.

The ride to the hospital was tense and he couldn't stop the feelings of anger, confusion and fear whirling around inside him. He felt like he was going to burst at any moment. They pulled up at the hospital and all he could do was hold his sister's hand as they wheeled her into the accident and emergency department.

They called down a cardiothoracic surgeon and Thomas felt foolish standing outside the pod, not being able to do what he was good at. This was the one time his medical training was useless, because there was nothing he could do to help.

And for the first time in a long time he understood what his patients' families went through. He always had that sense of sympathy and connection with them because of what had happened to his mother, but he forgot what it felt like to feel completely helpless, and he didn't like it one bit.

Geraldine stood back as the cardiothoracic surgeon stepped in and started checking the pacemaker. Scans were being ordered. Geraldine was just a cardiologist. She had hospital privileges, but she wasn't a surgeon; didn't have the training.

She glanced back at Thomas through the glass of the trauma pod and he could see the sympathy in her eyes. He went to the doorway.

"Do you want me to leave?" she asked.

"No. Please stay with her. I know there's not much you can do, but it would make me feel better if you stayed with her. Zoe trusts you. She came to you. Not me."

And it killed him to admit it.

"She didn't want to worry you," Geraldine said, trying to ease his concern, but it didn't work.

"I would've rather known. This is a thousand times worse than not knowing."

She shook her head. "I'm sorry, but I couldn't tell you. Doctor-patient confidentiality."

And of course she was right. Geraldine had been just as stuck as him. In the heat of the moment he had been looking for someone to blame, but Geraldine couldn't have told him even if she'd wanted to.

"Please stay. For me. I need you to stay." His heart was tearing in two, waiting for her answer, and for putting his heart on the line, asking her to stay for him, but he needed her. Which terrified him.

Geraldine nodded. "I will. Of course I will."

Geraldine stood by helplessly while the cardiothoracic surgical registrars did their work in the cath lab, but she'd promised Thomas that she would stay with his sister the whole time. She felt a little bit foolish, standing off to the side in a ball gown, but after a bit she didn't care. She'd reminded herself that she'd done more embarrassing things in her younger days. This was nothing. She was doing this for her colleague.

Possibly her friend?

And she was doing this for her patient above all.

She'd seen the hurt in Thomas's eyes. She knew how much he cared for his sister and it broke her heart that this had had to happen. Zoe was too young to have this kind of thing happen to her, but then again she thought that about all her pediatric heart patients.

They were too young to have broken hearts, as it were. They didn't deserve it, which was why she wanted to become a cardiologist. To save lives.

It was why she'd wanted to become a cardiothoracic

surgeon. Only her foolish dealings with Frederick had ruined all that. She'd allowed her emotions to rule her instead of her head.

And when she and Thomas had been in that alcove together, she'd wanted him to kiss her. She had foolishly allowed her emotions to drive her decisions. And she was mad at herself for that. She was so weak.

She wasn't going to let another man get in the way of her career again.

She was here to be a cardiologist. That was it. There would be no running away this time, because she wasn't going to make the same mistake twice.

Right now while they were doing a heart catheterization to repair the damage to Zoe's pacemaker she wished she had her surgical training so that she could help Zoe, to ease Thomas's worry. She knew how to do this. She was good at heart catheterizations. Zoe was her patient and she should be the one in there.

Only she wasn't. And it was all her own fault.

Thomas was pacing in the hallway. The pain etched on his face was more than Geri could bear. She'd never seen him like this. He'd always had that air of devil-may-care, always joking, always smiling, always a twinkle in his eye. There were also times he was so arrogant it set her teeth on edge, but this was different. She felt bad for him. She felt bad that this was happening to him. Her friend. That's all he was. Her first real friend in London.

Geri took a deep breath and stepped out into the hallway. Thomas came rushing over to her, pain and worry etched into his face.

"Well?" he asked.

"They are doing the heart catheterization right now. The pacemaker was fine when I checked it four days ago. The computer ran a perfect test. She's had that pacemaker since she was ten, there was nothing wrong with it."

Thomas cursed under his breath and ran his fingers through his hair. "Yes, but, like all technology, all machines can be faulty. They're not good enough."

"The heart catheterization will work. They'll repair the faulty wiring in the pacemaker. She won't need to have another one inserted again. She's going to be fine."

"How do you know that?" Thomas asked.

"You should know that. You're a surgeon. A heart surgeon even. She's in good hands."

"Who's doing the catheterization?"

"Dr. Sandler is doing it."

Thomas groaned. "Ugh."

"Is there something wrong with Dr. Sandler performing the procedure?" Geraldine asked.

"No. Nothing wrong. He's a good doctor."

"Then you shouldn't be worried."

"Well, I am worried," Thomas snapped. "Zoe's all I have left. My father is gone, my mother is gone… Zoe is all I have."

"I'm here," Geri said. "I promised you I wouldn't leave her side."

"Why are you doing this?" Thomas asked. "We're just colleagues. You've said so yourself several times."

"Yes, we're colleagues and this is what good colleagues do for one another. We're partners in a practice. I would hope when it came to my father you would do something to help."

Thomas's expression softened. "I wish I could do something, but cancer isn't my forte, unless it was cancer of the heart, but even then he wouldn't let me operate on him."

Geri cocked an eyebrow. "Why is that?"

Thomas chuckled. "Because we're too close. He's been my mentor. He was also my father's worst enemy."

She laughed. "Yes. Rivals who fought over my mother apparently."

"Right. I'm sorry for telling you that."

Geri shrugged. "If it's the truth, don't be sorry. It's too bad that my mother caused such a rift between your father and mine. My mother had a way of ruining so much."

"You don't think very highly of your mother."

"She didn't think very highly of me either. My childhood was very lonely, only I didn't have boarding school to escape to or a half sister to show affection to."

"We're pretty similar," he said quietly.

"How? We grew up in different worlds."

"We both had pretty crappy childhoods."

Geri chuckled. "That we did."

Thomas sighed. "Well, if you must know it wasn't just your mother that caused the rift between our fathers. My father was an Oxford man and your father was a Cambridge man. I believe they both were on the rowing teams and your father's team would often best my father's team. It enraged my father that your father seemed to beat him."

"Your father held a lot of grudges."

"There's a very old rivalry between the two schools."

She cocked an eyebrow. "I think it's more than that."

"I agree, my father was a jerk." Then they both laughed at that. "I'm surprised your father gave me the time of day, but he did. He's a good man, you know."

"I know," said Geri, her voice wobbling ever so slightly.

"He'll beat this. He'll come through," Thomas said.

Geri took his hand in hers and gave it a reassuring squeeze. "And Zoe will be fine."

She stared into his eyes and was completely lost at that moment. Her hand felt so tiny in his strong ones and she wanted to hold him closer. To comfort him.

He's not yours.

Thomas snatched his hand back and cleared his throat. He looked uncomfortable. "Thank you for being there with her."

"It's my pleasure. She's my patient."

"Sorry your night was ruined. It was your first social function and I know how much your father was looking forward to you going. He wanted to show you off."

"It's all right. This is why I became a doctor. This is what I'm passionate about, not dressing up in ball gowns and dancing. Though I wish I could've tried some of those desserts."

Thomas laughed. "They weren't that great."

"Oh, come on, they were traditional Victorian Christmas desserts. I mean the whole theme was Victorian Christmas."

He rolled his eyes, but smiled at her. "You and Christmas."

"You know you're a bit of a Grinch," she teased.

"A what?"

"Don't you remember watching that cartoon as a child?"

Thomas shook his head. "I didn't watch cartoons as a child. Remember, I'm not a big Christmas fanatic like you are."

"You mean you've never seen *How the Grinch Stole Christmas* with Zoe?"

"No," he said. "In her younger days, before Zoe's mother joined Doctors Without Borders, Zoe spent Christmases with her. I've only had her at Christmas for the last three years and she was never really interested in watching cartoons by the time she came to me."

"Well, you're maybe going to have to rectify that. She's going to need a few days of bed rest," Geri said.

"I wouldn't even know where to begin with Christmas specials."

"Well, maybe I'll help with that. I have an extensive collection."

"How extensive?" he asked carefully.

"Quite extensive. I have cartoons, funny movies and those Christmas specials that bring a tear to your eye."

"Ugh," he said dramatically. "That doesn't sound painful at all."

"How can you not like a big fat orange cat bringing Christmas to a grandmother? Or a family whose Christmas goes absolutely and completely wrong in a house full of annoying relatives? Or those old classic movies where the Christmas carols were written? Bing crooning away those familiar tunes."

He smiled and she melted slightly. What was she doing? Why was she still trying to get closer to him? Why couldn't she keep away from him? They were colleagues, partners, and that was it. They could be nothing more. She didn't want to be his friend outside work. She didn't want to be anything other than a medical associate. That's all she was here for. She wasn't here for anything else. And he was definitely not the right man for her.

He was a duke. She was struggling with the idea of being a lady, an heiress. She didn't want any part of that life.

Thomas is more than just his title. Just like you are.

"Well," she said, clearing her throat. "I'd better get back in there and see how it's going. You should get some rest in the doctors' lounge. It might be some time yet."

"No, I can wait it out in the hallway here. I'm not leaving her side. As I said, she's all that I have."

Geri nodded and headed back into the heart catheterization lab. All she had was her father. Her mother was off goodness knew where and doing who knew what, they had never really been close. Though she wasn't close to her father yet. She enjoyed being in his company, he was a brilliant physician and she hated seeing him sick. Yet, if he had been on this table, would she be as worried? Would she feel as hurt?

She wasn't sure. It had been so long since she'd cared about anybody. She wasn't even sure that she could anymore. She wasn't sure that she could open up her heart to anyone ever again.

CHAPTER EIGHT

I'M JUST CHECKING up on my patient, that's all.

Geri took a deep calming breath as she stared up at the impressive frontage of Thomas's Notting Hill home. Thomas had taken a week off three days ago when Zoe had been released from the hospital and she was worried about them both. Worried about Zoe's pacemaker failing again, even though the heart catheterization had been successful, and worried about Thomas too. He'd been so torn up over his sister.

She wanted to make sure they were both all right and, truth be told, she missed seeing Thomas every day. Missed his quips, his cheeky smiles. He'd only been in her life a handful of days and she was already missing his company. The thought scared her and Geri almost turned back.

You're checking on your friends. Nothing more.

She'd made up her mind to check on them on Saturday as the practice was closed, and had decided to bring over some of her favorite Christmas movies to lend to Zoe and Thomas. And as she stared up at his home she saw it looked sadly bereft of any Christmas fanfare. Thomas hadn't been kidding when he'd said he didn't make a big deal out of Christmas.

All around his home, other homes and shops were getting ready to welcome Christmas. All except Thomas's, which looked cold, dark and dreary. Not a single wreath, which was a pretty sad state for a duke.

She pushed the buzzer on the gate.

"Hello?" Thomas's voice sounded tired and a bit annoyed.

"It's me, Geraldine Collins. From the practice."

You idiot. He knows who you are.

"Yes. Geraldine Collins from the practice. How are you?" He was teasing her; she could hear the humor in his voice.

"Can I come in or are we going to conduct our entire conversation at your gate while your neighbors stare at me?"

"That is true. I'm most certain they'll stare at you."

"Thomas, are you going to leave me out here?"

"I might. This is fun."

Infuriating man.

"Fine. I'll leave, you cruel man."

She could hear his deep chuckle. "I love that adorable little accent you take on when you get annoyed."

"Aye, well, you'll be hearing it often, then, you fiend."

"All right, I'll let you in."

Then there was a buzz as the gate was unlocked. She pushed it open and then shut it again to lock it once more. She walked up the cleared flagstone path and Thomas met her at the front door.

He was a wearing jeans and a casual deep blue shirt that was open at the neck. His hands were thrust deep in his pockets. Even though he was casually dressed, it was business casual attire and Geri felt instantly underdressed in her leggings, long oversize sweater, ski vest and clunky boots. Her knit cap was a bit battered and her scarf didn't match it.

She felt positively dowdy in his presence suddenly.

It's not like you're staying. You're here to do a quick check, drop the movies and leave.

"What a pleasure to see you here," he said cordially. He looked her up and down and when his gaze landed on her big clunky boots a small smile twitched on his face. "Going hiking through some snowbanks today?"

"Ha-ha. They're warm." She held out the movies. "I brought Zoe some movies, since you're such a Christmas miser. I thought she'd enjoy these."

He took them. "Well, why don't you come in and say hello to her? She'd love to have a visitor. I have been a bit of a friend miser as well. I don't want her catching a cold or something that would be detrimental, given she's just had a heart catheterization."

"Sure. I would actually like to check on her. Father's been bugging me to swing by. He was worried about her, but he's not up for visiting either." She walked into his house and began to unwind her scarf and pull off her hat, trying to smooth down the static in her hair as Thomas shut the door.

"How is he feeling a week postchemo?" he asked.

"Tired," Geri said. "He goes for another treatment on Monday."

Thomas winced. "Not fun."

"No, it's not."

"Well, come upstairs. The family room is on the upper level, and that's where Lady Zoe is holding court at the moment on the couch."

Geri laughed and kicked off her boots, forgetting that she was wearing particularly ugly warm socks, the kind that separated the toes and were striped in rainbow colors. She'd meant to change them but had completely forgotten as she'd been running out the door.

Thomas cocked an eyebrow. "Interesting choice in socks, Lady Collins."

"Don't talk about eccentricities to me, Your Grace. You're the duke who lives in Notting Hill instead of on an estate, tending to your serfs and vassals."

"I have a Buckinghamshire estate, I just don't like it as much as here."

She followed him up the stairs to the next floor, where a cozy, plush sitting room area was. On the wall on the far side was a huge wide-screen television and facing that was an overstuffed, large couch, where Zoe was propped up surrounded by pillows and snuggled down in a blanket, watching a movie.

"Look who's come to see you, Zoe," Thomas said as they entered the room.

Zoe turned and smiled. "Dr. Collins!"

"I'm glad you're happy to see me. I'm sorry your brother now knows. I swear I didn't violate doctor-patient confidentiality."

She shrugged. "It was my own fault, I guess."

"It wasn't your fault," Thomas said. He handed her the stack of movies. "Geraldine has brought you some Christmas movies because she felt you were a bit deprived, given that I'm such a… What did you call me the other day?"

"Grinch," Geri said.

Zoe laughed. "This is wonderful. Can we watch one now?"

"I guess so," Thomas groaned halfheartedly.

She flicked through the movies. "*White Christmas*! I haven't seen this in so long."

"Good choice," Geri said. She stood up. "Well, I'd better head for home. I'm glad you're doing well, Zoe."

"Stay, Geraldine. If you don't have any plans, maybe we can order in some Chinese takeaways and watch *White Christmas* together." Zoe batted her puppy dog eyes in her direction, trying to play on her sympathies.

Geri glanced at Thomas. "If your brother doesn't mind?"

"No, I don't. And that sounds like a great plan." He smiled at her warmly. "I'll put in the order and you two get comfortable. Can I get you something to drink, Geraldine?"

"Tea would be lovely."

He nodded and then disappeared from the living room.

"I'm so glad you came, Geraldine. Thomas has been hovering over me like an overprotective hen. He carries me to bed at night. It's getting a bit much."

"Well, they did run the catheter up through your femoral artery. That's a main artery and prone to quick blood loss."

Zoe rolled her eye. "I know. My brother is a surgeon and he likes to tell me all that kind of stuff all the time. I think he and my mom both think I should enter the medical profession."

"It's not a bad profession to be in, but, then, I'm biased."

Zoe smiled. "Just like Thomas and my mother. I'm surrounded by physicians. If my father was still alive, he might not be pushing me so much."

"What was your father like?" Geri asked, curious about the previous Duke of Weatherstone. From what Thomas had said, he didn't sound like a nice man, yet had managed to sire two children who were warm and friendly.

Zoe shrugged. "He was okay. A bit distant, but pleasant enough to me. He was always angry that my mother didn't want to marry him."

"Why didn't she?"

"My mother knew his heart belonged to Thomas's mother and she didn't want to live in another woman's shadow. She also wanted to continue her work with Doctors Without Borders. Being the next Duchess of Weatherstone wouldn't have afforded her that luxury. My parents were pleasant to each other and Mom encouraged me to spend time with my father and Thomas."

"At least that's something. My mother didn't encourage any kind of relationship."

"Your father has always been very kind to me and my mother. I'm sorry you didn't have him when you were younger."

Zoe's words cut like a knife and tears stung Geri's eyes. No, she wasn't going to cry here now. She cleared her throat. "Do you mind if I check it? See if it's healed enough and give a second opinion?"

"No, I don't mind." Zoe flicked off the blanket. She was wearing a long flannel nightgown and ugly socks similar to hers.

Geri examined the wound. It was still raw and wasn't healing as fast as she would like, but it would hold.

"I think your brother should still carry you up flights of stairs. It's still healing."

Zoe groaned.

"Glad you see it my way. She didn't believe me," Thomas said, entering the room with a tea set on a tray.

Zoe stuck her tongue out at him.

"Not a good way for a proper lady to act, scamp," Thomas teased.

He poured everyone a cup of tea and then they all settled on the couch to watch *White Christmas*. It was one of Geri's all-time favorite Christmas movies. She loved the songs, the costumes and the dancing. The age difference between Bing and Rosemary was a bit too much May-December for her, but it was so minor it didn't detract from her love of the movie.

It was nice sharing it with Thomas and Zoe.

It was nice sharing this movie with someone, and having Chinese food and watching a movie on a comfortable couch was absolute heaven. This was even better than watching it alone. She was sharing it with friends. Which was what Christmas was all about.

She snuck a quick glance at Thomas. He seemed to be enjoying the movie and as if he knew she was watching him he glanced over and smiled back at her.

What're you doing here?

She didn't know. She shouldn't have stayed, but she also didn't want to leave. It was nice being with someone. She'd been alone for so long and though she'd been fine with that as it was what she was used to, she much preferred this.

When the final number came on Zoe sighed.

"I wish we had a Christmas tree like that," Zoe said.

"That's gigantic and a fire hazard," Thomas argued.

"It's no bigger than the one at the party the other night," Geri said.

Thomas glared at her. "You're not helping."

"All right, then, maybe not that big, but I would love to have a Christmas tree nonetheless. Let's go out and get a Christmas tree," Zoe begged. "Please?"

"You're not going anywhere," Thomas said. "So you're definitely not going out to buy a tree."

"You could," Zoe suggested. "You both could go out and get a tree and some decorations and then we can decorate it tonight."

"You're imposing a lot on Geraldine."

"She won't mind." Zoe winked at her.

Geri knew she should leave, but she was enjoying her time with Thomas and Zoe. It had been a long time since she'd enjoyed herself like this, where she felt a part of a family. Where she wasn't alone. It scared her a bit.

"I'd love to but—"

"No buts," Thomas said, and then he took her hand in his, sending a zing of warmth flooding through her veins at the simplicity of his touch. "We'd love to have you."

* * *

Thomas had known that Geraldine had been going to make an excuse to leave and he should've let her go, but he didn't want her to. He'd never seen *White Christmas* before. It was an okay movie, but it was the time with his sister and Geraldine, the quality time, that's what he cherished. It was nice and he wanted to savor it.

And he didn't want it to end.

He had no problem going out and getting a Christmas tree for Zoe, as long as Geraldine came with him. As long as she stayed and helped decorate it.

"Are you sure?" Geraldine asked.

"Of course he is," Zoe insisted. "Please go out and get a proper tree and decorations and we'll decorate it. It would be wonderful."

"I will on one condition. You rest," Geraldine said to Zoe, tucking the blanket around her.

"Deal."

"Oh, I don't think we should leave her alone, though," Geraldine said. "She's still recovering."

"We have servants. Our housekeeper, Mrs. Brown, would be happy to sit with her." Thomas grinned at her. "There's no getting out of it, Geraldine. You're the one who loves Christmas most out of the three of us and you're the best one to pick out the tree and decorations."

"I guess that's settled."

Thomas nodded. "It is. Portobello Road should have everything we require and it's not that far from here. We can walk. I mean, you do have the proper footwear for it."

Geraldine rolled her eyes. "Let's go, then, before you change your mind."

Thomas left the sitting room and arranged for Mrs. Brown to keep an eye on Zoe while he was out with Geraldine, and by the time he was done Geraldine was waiting in the foyer all bundled up again.

Thomas put on his ski jacket and a knitted cap with flaps. When he turned round Geraldine laughed at him.

"You don't look very stately, Your Grace."

"Neither do you, My Lady, but will that stop you from escorting me out on my errand?" He bowed and added a little flourish.

"Of course not."

They headed out of the house. It was dusk and the Christmas lights were starting to come on. It wasn't snowing, though, which was a shame, because for the first time in a long time he felt a bit excited about the prospect of Christmas.

Like a bit of that Christmas spirit he'd thought was long gone was coming back to life. It was nice. They walked along the street and headed toward Portobello Road, which was bustling and overflowing with street vendors, Christmas paraphernalia and shoppers.

"Where do we get a tree?" Thomas asked as they walked through the crowds.

"The vendor over there looks like he has some good trees." Geraldine paused. "I just thought of something. How are we going to get it back to your place?"

"We'll carry it. Come on, we're two strong and healthy doctors. I'm sure we can carry a tree a couple of blocks."

"Okay, so let's get some decorations and tinsel in the Christmas shop there and then we'll pick up the tree. We can't go shopping for decorations lugging an evergreen all over the place."

"Good plan."

They wandered into the little shop that was overflowing with gifts, confectionary and decorations. It was Christmas overload in there. Thomas felt a little bit overwhelmed and wanted to leave, but Geraldine was in her element.

He never seen her like this. Her green eyes were sparkling and she was grinning as she filled a basket full of gaudy decorations. This wasn't the cold, detached doctor he was used to. This was a totally different person and he liked this side of her. This was the side he'd known was buried under that cold facade. This was the real her that she was so desperately trying to hide, but he couldn't figure out why.

"Can't we keep to a theme?" Thomas asked.

"A theme? If this is your first Christmas tree, the theme should be fun. What were you thinking?" Geraldine asked.

"Simplicity." Thomas stared at a box of twinkle lights. "Just a tree and maybe some ribbon."

She frowned at him and then sang a song, "You're a mean one, Mr. Ashwood…"

He rolled his eyes. "Fine, but no flashing lights. I don't want to have a seizure every time I go into the sitting room."

Geraldine laughed. "Deal."

"And no ornaments that bark or meow Christmas carols."

"How about a singing fish?" she asked, and pointed to the abomination wearing a Santa hat on the wall.

"No. Definitely not." As if on cue, someone else in the store pressed the fish and it began to sing "Jingle Bells" like Elvis.

"Why Elvis?" Geraldine asked in horror. "That is awful."

"We need to get out of here before we find out how that monstrosity sings." Thomas pointed towards the very large reindeer head that was hanging on the wall, also adorned with a Santa hat.

"Agreed."

They purchased their lights and decorations and then headed out to pick out a tree. They found one with ease and the man tied it up for them. Together they hoisted it up and portaged it much like a canoe down Portobello Road back towards his home.

He took the back end, because Geraldine wasn't as tall as him, so he could kind of steer. The problem was a lot of the lower branches blocked her view, so he had to guide her through the streets, making sure she didn't crash into anything.

"I'm getting covered in sap!" Thomas shouted.

"You're not a sap," Geraldine's muffled voice said from under the tree.

"I didn't say that I was, I said I'm getting covered in it."

"Oh, well, that's part of the experience."

Thomas groaned, but chuckled to himself. He could imagine his father's horror if he were still alive to see his heir meandering down the street carrying a tree to decorate. His father hadn't liked tomfoolery or antics much.

And this would definitely be tomfoolery in his books.

They got everything back to his house and hoisted it up the stairs to the sitting room. It was a pain and there were pine needles all over the floor. Poor Mrs. Brown didn't look too pleased that the tree was shedding all over the place.

"It looks wonderful," Zoe said.

Thomas set it upright and Geraldine climbed out from under the tree, out of breath but still smiling. "Yes, it does look good. Do you have a tree stand so we can set it up?"

"A what?" Thomas asked.

Zoe was laughing and Geraldine looked horrified.

"A tree stand—you know, to hold the tree up so we can decorate it."

"We have one in the attic, Your Grace. Shall I get it?" Mrs. Brown asked.

"Yes, please, Mrs. Brown, and thank you."

Mrs. Brown nodded and hurried off to find the stand.

Thomas leaned the tree against the wall, praying that it wouldn't leak sap all over the place.

"You'll have to water the tree," Geraldine said.

"I have to water it?" Thomas asked. "This is becoming more of a nuisance."

"You don't want it to dry out, Thomas," said Zoe. "It could catch fire."

"Catch fire?"

Geraldine and Zoe were both laughing now at his expense and he couldn't help but laugh too.

"Next year I want one of those trees that you pop open like an umbrella and it's all decorated for you and doesn't shed. Low-maintenance tree."

"Where's the fun in that?" Geraldine asked as she began to take the ornaments out of the bag so Zoe could look at them.

"The simple things in life, Geraldine, bring me the greatest pleasure."

She just shook her head at him.

Mrs. Brown returned with the antique tree stand and Thomas went about setting up the tree. That involved some more cursing and more jokes at his expense, but it was worth it to see Zoe really enjoying herself. To see her lit up like he hadn't seen her in a long time.

When he'd almost lost her that night when her pacemaker had stopped working, he had been so terrified. Zoe was the only happiness he had in his life. Cassandra had brought him that joy too, for a short while, but it could never have lasted. And he would never know the loving family he had dreamed of as a kid. He lived with it and didn't mourn what he didn't have. Yet today with Zoe and Geraldine he felt something akin to that and he realized that maybe he'd been too hasty in his decision to never let another person in.

No. You made the right decision. It won't always be like this.

Which was true. Zoe would go back to boarding school and eventually her mother would come home from her time in Malawi. A couple more years and Zoe would be a legal adult and making her own way in the world.

He didn't even know what Geraldine wanted. All he knew about her was that she was completely focused on her career and didn't seem at all interested in pursuing anything with him.

This moment would end, because that's all that it was. Just a moment.

Geraldine began to decorate the tree and he stood off to the side, watching as Zoe handed her different ornaments and gave her suggestions on where to place them. Being around Geraldine like this caused him to let his guard down.

And it scared him that she got through to him so easily.

What was it about her?

He had to get out of there. "I need to make a couple of phone calls. You two carry on."

Zoe frowned. "Now?"

Thomas nodded. "Yes, now, I'm afraid."

"Oh, well, the decorating is done and I should really get back home." Geraldine picked up her coat. "I'll see you at work on Monday. Zoe, enjoy the rest of the movies."

"I will, Geraldine. Thank you."

Geraldine nodded and stopped in front of him. "Thank you for the lovely time."

"My pleasure. I'll see you out."

You're a fool, Thomas Ashwood.

He ignored that other part of him that told him to pull Geraldine into his arms and kiss her, because he couldn't remember the last time he'd had this much fun.

Only he resisted as he opened the door for her. "Would you like me to drive you home?"

She shook her head. "No, I can take the tube back to Holland Park. See you Monday."

Thomas watched her walk down the path and through the gate. He stepped outside so he could see her head down the darkened street, heading toward the Underground station.

A bloody fool.

CHAPTER NINE

"WILL I BE in here over Christmas?" Lord Twinsbury demanded. "I can't be in here over the holidays."

"I'm afraid so," Thomas said as he finished his examination. "You're not healing as quickly as I'd like and you're still not ready to go home. You've had two open heart surgeries in the course of a couple of weeks. You need to stay in the hospital. So I'm afraid you'll be here for Christmas."

"Blast, I didn't want to miss the carols from King's College at Cambridge. It's important I attend."

"Understandable, but you're staying put."

Lord Twinsbury groaned. "You, of course, wouldn't understand. You're an Oxford man."

"Oxford or Cambridge makes no difference. You're recovering from surgery." Thomas leaned over. "Oxford is the far superior university anyway. You should know that."

"Young pup, if I weren't laid up…"

Thomas cocked an eyebrow. "You'd do what? Tan my hide? I think I can outrun you."

Lord Twinsbury huffed grumpily.

There was a knock at the door and Thomas turned to see Geraldine standing there. It had only been a couple of days, but his heart skipped a beat seeing her standing there in her business clothes and her pristine white lab coat.

"Am I interrupting?" she asked.

"Ah, now there's a sight for sore eyes!" Lord Twinsbury exclaimed with delight.

"Lionel, you flatter me," she said sweetly.

"Nonsense, you're a damn sight better than the duke here," Lord Twinsbury grumbled.

"That's Mr. Ashwood, my lord," Thomas corrected him.

"Can I speak with you, Mr. Ashwood, about a case?" Geraldine asked.

"Of course." He was glad to get away from Lord Twinsbury's complaining.

"Please come and see me afterward, my lady. Your visits make my day."

Thomas rolled his eyes.

"I will try, Lionel." Geraldine shut the door when Thomas was in the hall. "I'm sorry for pulling you away from your rounds, but I had a referral from a general practitioner in Aylesbury of a pregnant woman who has suffered a myocardial infarction."

"Your mother is dead, Thomas. So is the baby. They're gone and crying won't bring them back."

His father's harsh words haunted him. It had been at that moment his father had turned his back on him. Resented him for being like her. All Thomas had wanted was the comfort of his father when his mother had died, but he'd been denied it. Instead he'd been sent to boarding school. The day his mother had died had been the day he'd really lost both of his parents.

There had never been a chance for him or his father to make things right between them. The day Zoe had been born with the atrial septal defect and had almost died, his father had tossed him out of the room.

"Haven't you haunted me enough?"

It was almost as if his father had been blaming him for Zoe almost dying at birth. It's why Zoe's mother had walked away from his father and instead had became the surrogate of the parent he'd never had. His father had re-sented him for that too.

And they'd never had a chance to resolve anything. His father had hated him until the day he'd died, when Zoe had been ten.

At least his father had loved Zoe. That was at least something. Her life wasn't as devoid of love as his had been.

"I'm sorry?" Thomas said. His father's voice had drowned out Geraldine's words. The moment she'd mentioned a pregnant patient who had suffered a myocardial infarction he'd been taken back to that terrible day long ago when his father had told him his mother wasn't coming home.

"How is she?"

"I don't know, other than stable. She's in an ambulance on the way here. She's too far along in her pregnancy to be flown in. She's thirty-one weeks and could be on the verge of pre-eclampsia as well. They're trying to keep the baby in there as long as possible, but I have Obstetrics on standby as well."

"What is their plan?"

"Save the baby and then assess the mother."

Thomas nodded. "I can have my fellow finish rounds on my surgical patients and I'll go down to Accident and Emergency and wait for her arrival."

"Thank you. Hopefully she won't need extensive surgery on her heart."

"She'll need a heart catheterization, that much I know. I need to see the extent of the damage, but I want to be in that operating theater to watch her vitals."

"Yes, that's what the obstetric team is hoping for. As she's my patient now, I insisted on you taking care of her. I hope you don't mind."

"Mind? No, that's why we're in practice together."

"Yes." She glanced down at her pager. "They'll be arriving shortly. Shall we?"

"Let's go."

Thomas led the way down to A and E. The obstetrics team was standing by. They were going to deliver that baby so that Thomas could take over.

Focus.

This situation wasn't as dire as his mother's had been. His mother's heart attack had been fatal and his brother had been too young to survive outside the womb at twenty-one weeks. Even now, with all the technological advances, babies still rarely survived if they were born that early.

At least this patient's baby was thirty weeks. Still premature, still a fight ahead, but the percentages on surviving were far greater than they'd been thirty-odd years ago.

The ambulance pulled up and they went to work. Geraldine met the paramedics and the general practitioner, who had ridden with his patient from Aylesbury. He was explaining the situation to Geraldine, which was good. Then he could focus on taking care of the patient's heart as the obstetrics team dealt with the baby.

"She had another heart attack, minor, but another nonetheless on the way here. Her blood pressure is far too high to have flown her in." Thomas heard the general practitioner say.

"We need to get this baby out of her so I can address her heart," Thomas said above the din.

"Get her to a theater now," Mr Jones, the obstetrician, shouted to a resident. "Have the team prepare for a crash C-section."

Thomas took her blood pressure and it was dangerously high, the heart sounding like it was fighting to pump blood through her body. Even if they had stabilized her, the baby wouldn't survive with the mother's heart struggling so much.

From what he was seeing, she needed open heart surgery and she needed it now. Her heart was failing. It sounded like an enlarged heart. Cardiomyopathy.

Damn.

They rushed her to the operating theater and he set up all his monitors, the crash cart ready and standing by. It wouldn't take long to get the baby out and that was a blessing, especially if he needed to get in there and massage the heart or shock the mother's heart back into rhythm.

This operating theater didn't have a gallery, because no one needed to witness this. This was a possible tragedy in the making, but he wished that Geraldine was beside him. Right now he was a horrible mess of emotions.

Live. Just live.

Instead of his patient on the table, he saw his mother.

"Thomas, I love you." His mother's voice was in his head as he watched his patient. He hadn't heard his mother's voice in so long. He'd thought he'd forgotten it, but it came to him now and he closed his eyes, listening to the heart monitor. Willing his patient to live.

Live.

The jostling from the C-section played merry havoc with the heart monitors, but so far she was not having another heart attack. Which was good. In less than five minutes he heard the tiny wail of a premature boy as he was lifted up and placed into the hands of the waiting pediatric team.

Thomas smiled behind his mask and then whispered to his patient, who was under anesthesia, "It's a boy. You have a boy, you need to pull through."

"How is her heart, Mr. Ashwood?" Mr. Jones asked.

"Stable for now, Mr. Jones."

Mr. Jones nodded and continued his work on their patient. At least the baby was out and had a good fighting chance to survive. Thomas's job was making sure that the mother also had a fighting chance.

He was going to save that baby boy's mother, because he'd been unable to save his own.

Geraldine saw that Thomas was still sitting in the room of Mrs. Rimes, their patient who had been pregnant and who'd suffered two heart attacks.

"How is she doing?"

Thomas looked up. "Stable. She had massive damage to her heart and has severe cardiomyopathy. At least with the delivery of the baby she won't succumb to eclampsia."

"What do you think it was?"

"Arrhythmogenic right ventricular dysplasia."

"You're certain?"

He nodded. "She's at a risk for the rest of her life. When she recovers from her surgery I'll speak to her about her options, in particular implanting a device that will shock her heart should it happen again. And it will happen again."

"Poor woman."

Thomas got up and walked out of her room, shutting the door. "How is the baby?"

"Doing well," Geraldine said.

"Good." He scrubbed a hand over his face.

"Are you okay?"

"No, it hits a little too close to home for me. All I could hear was my father's voice in my head, telling me my mother was dead, when you came to tell me about our patient."

Geraldine reached out and touched his arm. She could see his pain again. Like the pain he'd had when Zoe had been in the heart catheterization lab. She couldn't even begin to comprehend what he was going through.

"I need to get a coffee. Would you care to join me?" Thomas asked.

"Of course." They walked toward the small coffee shop that was located in the hospital. Thomas ordered them a couple of cups of coffee and they sat down at a table. It wasn't busy in the coffee shop and that was fine by her.

"I'm so sorry this situation reminded you of your mother," she said.

"It's why I became a heart surgeon. I think we all have a reason why we become what we become. Why did you become a cardiologist? Was it because of your father?"

"No," Geri said quickly. "No, not at all." She was uncomfortable discussing this. It was hard to step back and not be in the operating theater where she belonged. She felt useless and helpless. Almost worthless.

Thomas cocked his head to one side. "You said that with such conviction."

"Well, I didn't know about him and he didn't know about me until last year. No, my decision to be a cardiologist was because I wanted to save lives. But I'm not cut out for the operating theater."

"I disagree," he said.

"Why?"

"You're stronger than you give yourself credit for."

Geri wished she could believe that. "Well, it wasn't in the cards."

And she hoped that would stop the conversation.

"I'm surprised that you didn't become a surgeon."

I wanted to.

"I wasn't made for surgery."

Liar.

"What makes you think that? You didn't shy away in the operating theater when Lord Twinsbury was having his surgery. You thought quickly with that suggestion about the umbilical vein. I think, given your drive, that you belong in the operating theater, as I've said before. I think you're made for it."

Geri sighed. "Well, it's a little too late for that. I'm a cardiologist and I'm taking over my father's practice."

"It's never too late."

"I'm happy as a cardiologist." She took a sip of her coffee. Then she changed the subject. "How is Zoe doing? Is she enjoying her Christmas tree?"

"She's doing well and, yes, she's enjoying her tree. I'm not, for the record."

Geri chuckled. "Why am I not surprised? How can anyone not enjoy a Christmas tree?"

"It sheds. It's worse than my grandmother's Pomeranian, which shed everywhere."

"How can a tree be worse than a dog?"

"It can." As he winked at her, his pager went off. "Our patient is awake and her husband has been waiting very patiently in the waiting room. I'll counsel them on the next steps."

"I look forward to reading your report so I can continue guidance on the matter as well."

Thomas nodded.

She should head back to the office. There was nothing more she could do here. She wasn't a surgeon. There were times she regretted running away, taking the easy way out, like now, and like what had happened with Zoe. But that was her burden to bear.

No one else's. It was all hers.

Despite what Thomas had said, it was too late for her to continue with her specialization. She would never be a surgeon. It's just the way it was and she was okay with that.

Though she had the feeling that Thomas didn't believe her.

And she didn't know why. It shouldn't matter to him. Why did he want her to become a surgeon anyway? There wasn't room in the practice for two surgeons. Did he want her to be competition?

Geri shook her head and threw her empty coffee cup in the garbage. She'd head back to Harley Street and wait for Thomas's report on their new patient, because when she no longer needed the surgeon that's when Geri had a chance to help save a life.

CHAPTER TEN

THOMAS RANG THE DOORBELL at Charles Collins's Holland Park townhome. He knew that Geraldine wasn't there, but it wasn't Geraldine who had asked him to come by. It had been Charles.

Why, he didn't know, but Charles had been most insistent that Thomas stop by while Geraldine was at work. And he was happy to oblige. He just hoped this wasn't some sort of cry off about his daughter, because there was no reason for that.

Wasn't there?

And the thought caught him off guard.

There was something he just didn't want to admit, but Geraldine had seen him at his most vulnerable lately.

And he desired her.

It was something more than a quick seduction game that he played time and time again, but what it was he didn't know and that thought unnerved him because he couldn't have her. He wouldn't put her through any more pain. She'd been through so much already.

"Thomas, come in." Charles opened the door and Thomas stepped past him into the foyer. Charles took his coat and hung it up. "Won't you join me in the sitting room?"

"Of course," he said as he followed Charles into the sitting room. "I get a lot of flak, you know."

"For what?" Charles asked, confused.

"For living in Notting Hill in a modest-sized home, but what I don't understand is why you don't get any flak for living in a town house?"

Charles chuckled. "Who says I don't? Then again, I'm not a duke. I'm so far down the list of succession that a lot of people would have to die before I even had sight of the throne and I'm glad of that. You, on the other hand, are definitely an eccentric."

"Why, thank you."

"Drink?" Charles asked.

"No, I have to make rounds at the hospital soon." Thomas sat down on the sofa. "I'd much rather have the drink. So if you have a mineral water with a twist of lemon that would be great."

"Of course." Charles poured it and handed Thomas the glass. Thomas noticed Charles's hand shook.

"Thank you. Are you sure you're quite well?"

"I'm sure." Charles sat down, ending that topic. "I heard about the pregnant woman."

"Yes."

Charles knew about his mother, but he didn't want to talk about that right now. "How can I help you, Charles?"

"Geraldine tells me you're aware that I have cancer."

"Yes, Charles. I drove her to the hospital when you collapsed during chemo."

"You haven't told anyone else?" Charles asked carefully. He was hedging.

"Of course not. Why are you so concerned with keeping it a secret from your colleagues, though?"

"Just privacy. I don't need a lot of bleeding hearts telling me that I'm in their prayers or giving me sympathetic looks. I don't need that. I don't deserve that after all my sins of the past."

Thomas chuckled. "My father wouldn't be giving you any."

Charles snorted. "Don't even start with me about your father, who would, by the way, not approve of you living in Notting Hill."

"It's why I live there." Thomas winked.

"You are like him in some respects. Cheeky and arrogant, but that's what makes you a brilliant surgeon."

"Thank you again. Why do I deserve so much flattery this afternoon?"

"Because my cancer has moved from my stomach. And don't say it, don't say you're sorry."

"Where is it?" Thomas asked, but he had an idea.

"The heart. My angiosarcoma is small, but it's there."

"Charles, angiosarcoma is spread from soft-tissue cancer."

"Yes, that's where it spread first. Stomach into the heart. I want you to take out as much of the tumor as you can. I know it's not possible to take it all out and I know it's likely to come back, but I want a fighting chance and you're the most talented surgeon to do it."

Thomas wanted a drink as it all sank in. Charles was dying now. Previously he was battling cancer, but angiosarcomas were almost always fatal. In cases of malignancy the cancerous tissue had to be removed, but with a border of cancer-free tissues with good margins. It was almost impossible to do that with a heart.

And he couldn't operate on Charles because he thought of him as a sort of father figure. He respected him too much. He couldn't do it. Only he had to do it. His survival rates for this kind of surgery were the highest in London.

He wouldn't leave Charles high and dry.

"Does Geraldine know?" Thomas asked quietly.

"That it's spread? No. She doesn't and you're not to tell her. She needs to concentrate on work. I won't burden her with this."

"How are you burdening her? You're her father."

Charles's expression was weary. "Yes. In name, but... too much time was lost between us. I'm just looking for a bit more. You have to do the surgery for me."

"You told me you never wanted me to operate on you." It was a flimsy excuse.

"You're the only one who can. Your success rates are higher than most."

"Charles, they may be a bit higher, but angiosarcoma still ends up the same."

"Death, I know. I'm just asking for some more time. Time to get to know my daughter. I have a bit more living I have to do."

Thomas's heart sank. There was no way he could turn this down. "I'll do it, but I won't keep it secret from Geraldine. She needs to know what's happening."

"You're a thorn in my side, Thomas. You know that?" Charles grumbled.

"I know, but now I'm your surgeon and you have to listen to me. Oh, the power I'll wield."

"Ha-ha." Charles leaned back in his chair. "I'll tell her, but after the country party this weekend. If I tell her now she'll try to get out of it."

"You're not going to that? It's in Buckinghamshire and you're not well enough to travel."

"I know, which is why I'm hoping you'll go in my place."

Thomas shook his head. "No, you know my history with the Ponsonby family. You know that they're Cassandra's in-laws. I will not go there."

"Then I won't tell Geraldine about my angiosarcoma.

Take her to Buckinghamshire to the Ponsonby winter party or I won't breathe a word about my condition."

"That's absolute blackmail."

Charles grinned. "I know. Didn't Zoe want to attend that event?"

Thomas groaned. "All right, all right, I'll escort Geraldine to that event. Zoe can't go because she's still recovering from her own surgery. I won't have her traipsing around a winter garden party and being exposed to germs. Not in her fragile state. She can stay at home."

"Thank you, Thomas. Geraldine has so much to learn about our world."

"I hate to break it to you, old man, but I don't think she particularly cares about it."

"I know, but when I go she'll inherit everything, including my seat in the House of Lords. It's tradition, and I want someone I can trust to show her the ropes."

"I'll try, Charles. I will."

"That's all I ask." Charles sighed. "Actually, that's not all."

"Oh?" Thomas asked.

"You have my blessing. Not sure if you know that."

Thomas was confused. "To perform the surgery? I certainly hope so since you've just asked me."

"No, to date Geraldine." Charles scrubbed his hand over his face. It was apparently hard for him to talk about this.

"We're friends, Charles."

Charles shot him a disbelieving look. "I think it's more than that. You care for her, you're attracted to her, and I want you to know in case anything happens to me that you have my blessing. Just because you're your father's son, it doesn't mean I disapprove of you."

Thomas sighed. "Charles, I appreciate it, but… I have hypertrophic cardiomyopathy."

Charles was shocked. "Has it progressed?"

"No, I mean I'm a carrier."

"Then what is the holdup?" Charles asked, confused. "You're a carrier, but it might not amount to anything."

"Heart conditions are in my family. Look at my mother, father and Zoe. I can't do that to her."

"So you do care for her."

Thomas shook his head and stood. "I have to get back to the hospital. Thank you for the drink."

He couldn't talk about this, because it didn't matter if he did care for Geraldine. Nothing could happen. He wouldn't do that to her. Even with Charles's blessing, he just wouldn't put Geraldine's heart in danger.

Charles sighed. "I'll let you get to your rounds."

"Sounds good. I'll book your preoperative assessment and your surgery. The quicker I get in there the better margins I can get. Angiosarcomas grow very fast."

Charles nodded. "I know. Thank you."

"Of course, Charles. I'll show myself out." Thomas grabbed his jacket and then headed back into the street. He wondered how Geraldine was going to react when she found out and he was annoyed that Charles wasn't going to tell her unless he took her to that ridiculous winter garden party.

Now he felt an inkling of what Geraldine must've felt when she'd been unable to tell him about Zoe and the pacemaker.

He cursed under his breath and scrubbed a hand over his face. Families. They were too bloody complicated.

Charles and Geraldine aren't your family, though.

He really didn't want to go to that garden party in Buckinghamshire. He always avoided that party because he had no wish to see Cassandra ever again.

Not after she'd used him.

She wanted to be connected to an aristocratic family who was just that. Aristocratic. Maybe they had a job like barrister or solicitor, even banker, but she'd made it perfectly clear she didn't want a duke who was a surgeon and absolutely committed to his work.

There had been many times she'd been angry he'd missed some kind of function because a patient had been in need.

"Have someone else do it! You're the Duke of Weatherstone. You promised you'd be there."

"I'm well aware of my title, Cassandra, but first and foremost I'm a surgeon. My patient needed me."

"Is this how it's going to be? You're going to leave me high and dry at social functions because someone needs surgery?"

"Yes. Someone's life is more important than a party. I'm a surgeon first, Cassandra, and a duke second."

That had been the argument that had ended it all, although the relationship had been on its last legs ever since he'd explained that he was at risk of heart problems.

It was his fault. He'd chosen his career over love. And when he had started to date again, he'd soon learned that most women were like Cassandra. No one understood his passion for medicine.

Except Geraldine.

Yes, Geraldine understood it, but he wasn't completely sure how dedicated she was because he knew that she wasn't completely satisfied with being a cardiologist.

Why is it your concern? It's her life.

And he didn't know why he was so concerned about it. Geraldine was nothing more than a work friend.

Is she?

"That's a nasty angiosarcoma." Geraldine didn't mean to sneak up on Thomas, but he'd been so absorbed in the MRI of a nasty-looking cancer of the heart that he hadn't heard her come into his office.

He clicked the image closed on his computer and spun around, looking put out that she'd sneaked up behind him.

"Geraldine, I didn't hear you knock."

"I did knock, but you didn't answer and Mrs. Smythe told me you didn't have a patient so I thought it was safe for me to come in. I can see now why you didn't hear me knock. That was an impressive angiosarcoma."

"Yes," Thomas said evasively. "It doesn't look good."

"Have you told the pátient about it?" She asked taking a seat.

"The patient knows, but still wants me to proceed with the surgery." Thomas didn't look her in the eye and she had the distinct feeling he was hiding something from her.

It's not your concern.

"Hopefully you can get good margins but with that kind of tumor—"

"I know," Thomas said, cutting her off. "Is there something I can help you with, Geraldine?"

"Yes, I'm hoping you don't mind crying off this weekend garden party. I just don't want to go. I can spend the day in the office and Father will be none the wiser."

"You're not crying off. If I have to go, you have to go," he said sternly.

"If I don't go, why do you have to go? Father told me you didn't want to go either. I thought you were sympathetic to my plight."

Thomas chuckled. "I am, or usually I would be, but your father will have his spies out and I think it's better we go. It'll make him happy."

Geraldine groaned. "You're right. He'll have his spies. Who has a garden party in the middle of December anyway?"

He smiled. "The *ton* are an eccentric group of partygoers. Any excuse for a function or showing off."

"I'm surprised you don't throw a party to show off."

"My father used to, but they weren't my cup of tea. Of course, he would have functions at the family estate in Buckinghamshire. I live in Notting Hill."

"What happened to the estate?"

"It's still there. I rent it out occasionally, and part of it is open for tours. People tour the home and the gardens."

"Really, one day I would love to see where you grew up."

"Well, we can go tomorrow after we make our perfunctory rounds at the garden party."

Now she was intrigued. "That makes going to this garden party almost worth it."

He leaned across the desk, his hands folded. "And going with me isn't worth it?"

"I think it'll be entertaining," she teased.

"That's it?"

She shrugged. "What more do you want?"

"Touché."

"What time are you going to pick me up?"

"I have to drive?"

"I don't have a car. Remember, I take the Underground regularly."

"Hmm, how convenient." Then he grinned. "I'll pick you up tomorrow at ten in the morning. If we get to the garden party unfashionably early then we can probably make the last tour of my childhood home."

"I don't get a private tour?"

"Oh, you want a private tour?" His voice was husky and she realized she was treading on dangerous ground. She still remembered those women talking at that party about how the Duke of Weatherstone was a womanizer.

"No, I'll just stick with the standard one, thank you very much." She got up. "I'll leave you to your angiosarcoma. If you need any... What am I saying? I can't help you with that."

"You could if you were a surgeon."

It was a barb. "Why are you so obsessed with me becoming a surgeon?"

"Only because I think you'd be brilliant at it."

A warm flush spread across her cheeks. "Well, I'm not. I'll see you tomorrow."

She got out of his office as quickly as she could. She didn't want to discuss her being a surgeon anymore. It wasn't any of his business.

What was done was done. She was happy with her lot in life.

Are you?

And the answer was simple. She wasn't, but she was too scared to change it.

CHAPTER ELEVEN

"YOU CAME WITH the Duke of Weatherstone?"

Geri had been accosted by another group of ladies. It seemed that at the Gileses' party she had been seen with Thomas on the dance floor and slinking off to the alcove. He'd warned her that night he was giving her a reputation and he was right. The groups who had slighted her before suddenly couldn't let her be.

She was the new flavor of the month, it seemed.

"Yes. I did." It seemed like every time she ran into a new group of people at this garden party and they discovered she'd come with Thomas they were in a bit of shock.

"Thomas Ashwood?" another woman asked, that same dumbfounded look on her face.

"Yes. Is there another Duke of Weatherstone?" Geri was secretly enjoying this. She glanced across the room and could see Thomas engaged in a discussion with another group of people. As if he knew she was looking at him, he looked over and smiled, winking mischievously as if he was in on the joke. She wished for a moment that they were alone. She really hated these social gatherings.

"He's a bit of a womanizer," Mrs. Ponsonby, the hostess, said. "A love-them-and-leave-them type. My sister Harriet was his last victim—last winter, I believe. She wanted marriage, though, and he, of course, won't marry. So she moved on to someone more suitable."

"So I've heard, but I assure you there's nothing untoward about our relationship. We work together."

There were a few disbelieving glances exchanged.

"That's what he wants you to think and then the next thing you know he's taking you on a tour of his estate and you're in his bed."

"Oh, yes," another woman sighed. "And what a wonderful place to be."

Geri's stomach knotted and she almost choked on the glass of wine she was taking a drink from. The women she was standing with continued to talk and all she could think about was the fact that after they left here they were going to see his estate.

She refused to end up in his bed, though. She refused to get involved with another coworker. Not after what had happened to her in Glasgow with Frederick.

Only that relationship had played out similarly. Colleagues then friends and then lovers before Frederick had dumped her for another surgeon, whom he'd ultimately ended up marrying.

And she had a sickening sense of familiarity.

Was Thomas doing the same thing?

"He's never been the same since Cassandra," Mrs. Ponsonby said.

"Pardon?" Geri realized that the other ladies in the group had wandered away and it was just her and Mrs. Ponsonby standing there now.

"Thomas and Cassandra Greensby were in a relationship at least seven years ago now. After Cassandra called it off Thomas began his womanizing ways. His father was none too pleased. I think that's what caused the late duke's heart attack."

Geri rolled her eyes. "I believe it was hypertrophic

cardiomyopathy that caused it. It's when the heart tissue thickens."

The other woman gave her a confused stare. "What?"

"Never mind." Geri shook her head. "Why did she break it off?"

Mrs. Ponsonby shrugged her shoulders. "I don't know. I just know that it absolutely crushed him."

Geri felt guilty that she was being made privy to this information, which was none of her business. It was up to Thomas to tell her these things and he hadn't, so clearly he didn't want her to know. Just like she didn't tell him the reason she hadn't pursued becoming a surgeon was because of Frederick. How he'd run the surgical program and she was a coward, not facing her broken heart and not becoming the surgeon she'd always dreamed of being.

Instead, she'd taken the offer of her father.

She never wanted Thomas to know that secret shame of hers and she was sure that he didn't want her to know about this Cassandra Greensby, whoever she was.

"Excuse me, Mrs. Ponsonby. I think I'll take a quick stroll around your lovely conservatory."

"By all means, do. I'm sorry your father couldn't be here. This is where he met your dear mother." Mrs. Ponsonby wandered off. She didn't correct Mrs. Ponsonby over calling her mother "dear." There was nothing dear about her mother.

"Although your mother was a party crasher."

"So I heard." And it was nothing surprising. Her mother had often crashed big formal events. It was embarrassing really.

Geri had no real interest in knowing about how her parents had met, she knew the stories, but the more she lingered at this party the more she wanted to go back to London, back to Holland Park and her bed. Just shut the world out for a couple of hours and lock away all these feelings that were getting stirred up in her today.

The conservatory was quite extensive, overgrown with lush tropical greenery and winding paths. It was like something that should be a tourist attraction. Other people wandered along the paths, drinks in hand, as they soaked up the sun filtering through the glass.

Geri found a quiet bench where she could sit and collect her thoughts and enjoy the rest of her glass of wine in privacy.

"There you are. I despaired of ever finding you in this jungle."

She glanced up to see Thomas standing in front of her. He was grinning from ear to ear.

"Blast, I thought I was better hidden," she teased.

He chuckled. "You sounded quite like Lionel there."

Geri couldn't help but laugh at that. "Well, he's a bit of a bad influence and every time I'm in the hospital he demands to see me. He's also demanding to know when he'll get out."

"I know," Thomas groaned. "And I've told him time and time again it won't be before Christmas, but apparently that's not the answer that he wants to hear."

"I don't blame him. He said he looks forward to the King's College Choir carols every Christmas Eve. He's never missed it."

"He will this year."

"I was thinking about taking him to it," she said offhandedly. "As his physician naturally."

"He's barely out of the intensive care unit and you want to expose him to all the germs and the draughts of King's College Chapel and take him over an hour away from the hospital? I think not."

"Maybe you're right."

"Of course I'm right. I'm always right." Thomas winked.

"I've been getting quite an earful about you," Geri teased.

"Yes. I'm sure that you have," he said. "I saw you were talking to our hostess. She's a busybody."

"She told me that you're going to seduce me when you take me out to your estate."

Thomas's eyes darkened a bit. "Would you like that?"

Yes.

"Not particularly."

"Ouch." He grabbed his chest. "You don't pull any punches, do you?"

"I'm sorry."

"You're completely not, because you're laughing about it."

"I swear I'm not." She took another sip of her wine. "When can we make an exit?"

"Oh, we're not leaving anytime soon. I'm going to drag out this event as long as I can since you're been so cruel to me." His eyes were twinkling and she gave him a little shove with her shoulder.

"Mrs. Ponsonby also mentioned this is the place my parents met."

"You say that with such apathy…"

"How my mother crashed a party. I guess it's good they met or I wouldn't be here."

"And for that I'm thankful."

Geri blushed at his compliment. "It's not like it was a great romance. They had a brief marriage and went their separate ways. I was born and my father never knew about me."

"No, I guess you really don't have much sentimental value placed on where they met, do you?"

"I would if they'd actually had some kind of romantic feelings about each other, but from what I understand from my mother it was just sex that attracted her to my father.

The marriage had been spur-of-the-moment, and the lust wore out eventually, but it resulted in me. That's what she said. I don't think she loved my father much either. No love lost there. And, frankly, thinking about my parents together…" She shuddered for effect and Thomas laughed.

"Yes. I understand. I like to think I was an immaculate conception."

She choked on her wine, trying not to laugh.

"Don't laugh at me," Thomas teased.

"You make it so easy, though." She smiled at him. "I can't remember ever laughing so much in my life."

"Well, at least I'm good for something. Did you ever get your father's side of the story?" Thomas asked.

"No. What does it matter? It's in the past. You can't change the past."

"You certainly can't," Thomas said wistfully. "Only I wish…"

"You wish what?" Geri asked as he trailed off, but he wasn't listening to her. He was staring at the woman and man who had entered the conservatory. The woman was stunningly beautiful, blonde, tall. Like a model.

And she couldn't help but wonder if it was a past conquest or perhaps Cassandra.

"Let's go," Thomas said quickly. He took her hand and pulled her to her feet.

"I'm good with that. I've had my fill."

Thomas didn't say anything but dragged her along the path away from the woman and the man she was with.

"Thomas?"

He stopped and Geri almost slammed into his back. She could hear him cursing under his breath and he turned around. Geri saw the tall blonde walking toward them.

"Cassandra," he said through gritted teeth. "How very nice to see you."

"I doubt that very much, Thomas." She turned to the man who was with her. "My husband, Lord Greensby."

Thomas nodded and then pointed to Cassandra. "May I present Lady Collins."

Cassandra was taken aback. "Lord Collins got married? And to a much younger woman, I see."

"I'm not his wife, I'm his daughter," Geri said. She already didn't like Cassandra on principle for breaking Thomas's heart, but other than her looks she didn't know what Thomas saw in her. She was downright snobbish.

The more she saw of this circle her father belonged to the less she liked it. She resented it, as well. Her father put so much stock in this world and for what? She didn't like the people she met.

Except Thomas.

And he was part of this. If the rumors were to be believed, he'd almost married someone like Cassandra. Was that what Thomas really liked? If so, she needed to put an end to this because she was never going to be like one of these women. She was never going to be so vain and shallow.

Her career came first.

"Oh, yes, I thought I heard something about that," Cassandra said flippantly. "I didn't really pay much attention to it. I am really surprised to see you here, Thomas. I never thought you would be at one of these functions again."

"I'm surprised that I'm here myself, to be honest," Thomas said, sounding completely bored.

"Why are you here?" Cassandra asked, and Geri sensed a faint sense of hope in her tone.

"I promised Lord Collins I would escort Lady Collins here. He's tied up at work."

"Doctors," she said with disgust.

"Do you have an issue with doctors?" Geri asked.

"Not in particular, but it's the weekend."

"So? Life and death don't stop at the weekend," Geri countered.

Cassandra's ice-blue eyes narrowed on her. "You're quite passionate about medicine."

"I'm a doctor as well."

"How droll. I've never heard of an heiress becoming a surgeon."

"Have you been living in a cave?" Geri was about to hit this woman, but Thomas squeezed her hand and she took a deep calming breath.

"If you'll excuse us, Cassandra. I have to take Lady Collins back to London." Thomas didn't wait for any more polite exchanges as he dragged Geri off. She set her empty wineglass on a tray a waiter held and followed Thomas to pick up their coats in the foyer.

Only when they were outside, waiting for Thomas's car to be brought round to the front door, did Thomas finally give a sigh, which sounded like one of relief, and then he chuckled.

"'Have you been living in a cave?' That was priceless. The look on her face." Thomas grinned at her and Geri couldn't help but laugh, as well.

"Well, I mean, honestly. A lot of heiresses have careers. Why does she find it so surprising?"

"Probably because she finds it horrifying," he replied.

"That I do believe."

Thomas's car appeared and he took his keys from the valet. They climbed into the car and Thomas drove away from the Ponsonbys' home.

"How do you know Cassandra Greensby?"

"I'm surprised Mrs. Ponsonby hasn't told you."

"She did," Geri admitted.

Thomas cursed under his breath. "I thought as much."

"Well, you dodged a bullet there."

Thomas didn't respond, but his hands gripped the wheel

tightly as they drove through a small village, whipping round a roundabout before turning down another small road.

"Are you taking me back to London? I do have a lot of work," she said.

"Oh, no, we're still going to my estate, but I promise you I won't act in any untoward fashion." He smiled.

"Good, I would like to see it. Father hasn't taken me to ours, not that it's large, just a manor house in Oxfordshire, but he rents it out."

Thomas nodded. "Yes, I know. I've seen it once and it's nothing too grand. His Holland Park home is much nicer, but as he's a member of the House of Lords he also keeps his estate."

"The House of Lords is sitting next week. I don't think he'll be making it, given his condition."

Thomas's heart skipped a beat and he hoped Charles had finally told Geraldine about the angiosarcoma. "Condition?"

"His chemotherapy. I don't think he's in any shape to attend a House of Lords session."

"Of course." Thomas sighed. For one moment he'd thought she knew about the angiosarcoma. If Charles lived up to his end of the bargain she would know soon enough.

"Are you going to go?"

"Good lord, no." Thomas winked at her and she smiled.

"You're an idiot, you know that?"

"Hardly." And he laughed. "No one has ever called me an idiot before."

"No one?" she asked in disbelief.

"I believe my father often referred to me as a buffoon but that's not the same thing."

"I think you'll find it is."

"I hope you don't mind, but my family estate will be covered in Christmas decorations. I know how you hate that."

Geri rolled her eyes. "Really?"

He shrugged. "I know it was a foolish thing to ask, but I didn't want you to be surprised by the extent of Christmas decorations at my home."

"I'm actually surprised at that," Geraldine said. "I didn't think you liked Christmas too much."

"I don't, but it brings in the tourists and the trust that runs the tours is all about bringing in the tourists. They love it. They've been trying to get me to come to a Christmas event—you know, Christmas luncheon with the Duke and all that. They've been trying for years, but I haven't been very interested."

Geraldine perked up. "That sounds like fun!"

"It's not really that much fun."

She grinned at him. "Well, I think it would be. Why don't you do it this year?"

"Maybe I will…"

The rest of the drive was pretty pleasant. They wound their way through back country roads far off the motorway until they came to a long winding road with signs that pointed to Weatherstone House.

Geri had been expecting something similar to her father's estate, which she had seen photographs of. She was in no way prepared for what she was looking at as they came up the long tree-lined drive, before coming to a clearing and getting a chance to see the house in all its glory.

The house was grand. It looked like something out of a Jane Austen movie. She wasn't expecting anything like this.

"This is your family estate. You told me it was just a small estate home."

"Did I?" Thomas asked, grinning.

"This is huge."

It was definitely bigger than her father's estate. She'd expected Thomas's home to be slightly bigger, she just wasn't expecting it to be *Mr. Darcy* bigger.

"Have I seen this in a television production?" she asked.

He shrugged. "Could be. It was used for filming for some Hollywood movies in the sixties and seventies. Some period pieces, I'm not quite sure what."

Thomas drove down a private driveway that was marked for family only and whipped around to the back of the house. When he parked the car and she got out she could see several cars, and that indeed the building was decked out in Christmas flair.

Dusk was starting to settle and the Christmas lights started to come on, thousands upon thousands of white Christmas twinkle lights. It was almost magical.

"We'll be just in time for the last tour," Thomas quipped cheerfully.

"Isn't this your home? Does it matter if we're in time for the last tour? Don't I get a private one?"

"Good point," he said, grinning. He took her hand. "Come on, then, you wanted to see my house."

"You offered."

"Right. And I promise no hanky-panky."

Geri's cheeks heated as he reminded her that he'd be good, even though she actually didn't want him to be.

She followed him into the back entrance, into the private part of the home.

"This is where I stay when I come here to manage some of the land and deal with the trust that takes care of the public part of the house and operates the tours, but for the most part I'm not here. This part is pretty boring, pretty modern. This is the part my father had redone, because he lived here the whole time there were tours running. He used to attend the events arranged for Christmas—luncheons with the Duke."

From everything that Thomas had said about his father, Geri could believe him doing that. "Did your mother enjoy attending the Christmas lunches with the Duke?"

He grinned and then laughed. "Yes, she did. In fact, it was her idea to start opening up the house for tours."

They walked through a few more doors and suddenly they were in the main foyer, which held a profusion of marble, gilt and had a high ceiling with a crystal chandelier in the very center. It reminded her of the home in Mayfair where they'd attended the Christmas social event the night Zoe's pacemaker had failed.

And like in that foyer, there was a huge tree here. It was bigger than the one in the Mayfair house and it was decked out in gold, reds and greens. It was the brilliant, rich colors that reminded her of Victorian Christmases. It was overwhelming. It was like she'd stepped back in time.

Art adorned the walls, and she could tell from a glance that some of the paintings were by the great masters. The winding staircase was breathtaking, its banister covered in garlands. If she closed her eyes she could imagine a Victorian lady coming down the stairs in a wide ball gown.

"It's not much, but it's sort of home," Thomas said self-deprecatingly.

"Not much? This is amazing."

"Well, they take good care of it. Come on, this way." He led her through double doors to the dining room, which was set out as if they were expecting a Royal visit. Porcelain dishes were laid out on a table that had to be at least forty feet long. It was decorated as if there was going to be a Christmas dinner. There was a lot of holly, ivy, garlands and pine boughs, as well as poinsettias, which Thomas said came from the hothouse.

There was even a Yule log, not burning but in the fireplace.

She craned her neck to look up at the painted ceilings. The walls were papered in a deep red and the frames of the portraits were gilt. Geri wandered over to one of the windows and looked out at the extensive parkland at the back of the house, where there was a large sweeping garden with a canal pond and fountain.

At that moment it felt like she'd been transported to a different world.

"How much land does your family own?"

"Why?" he asked. "Is that important to you?"

"No, of course not. I'm just curious. This place is huge."

He laughed again. "Yes, it's a large estate. Not as big as some, mind you, but quite extensive. There's an arboretum, woods and a sculpture garden. Honestly, I don't know what's back there anymore. I think there are stables, but I'm not sure. I'm not into horseback riding, as my forebears were."

"That's interesting. Men like you usually are."

"Are you?" he asked.

"No. I never had the opportunity to be around horses. Horses were a luxury for a girl growing up in a single income home in Glasgow. I didn't even know who my father was."

"So I can say the same about you. Usually aristocratic women love horseback riding."

"Do you own horses? Maybe you can teach me."

"I own some racehorses, but teach you to ride? I'm afraid I can't do that. Would you care to see more of the house?"

"Of course," she said.

Geri followed him into a library that had a vast collection of old books. Thomas showed her some first editions… Dickens and Austen to name a few. There were books that his family had been collecting since the time of King Henry VIII.

Some books were behind glass because they were so old they couldn't be handled without gloves.

"I'm really thankful for having parts of the house put into the care of the trust and offering tours. They can take care of all this properly."

"It's too bad you can't use this room anymore."

"I can," he said. "There are certain times of the year that the house isn't open to tours. I try not to touch the books, though, especially the very old ones. I don't want to damage them. Again, I'm very thankful the trust takes care of my family's history like this."

Eventually they wandered upstairs.

He opened a door. "This is a representation of what the duchess's room might've looked like at the turn of the last century."

Geri walked into a beautiful room that was Orient themed, which had been the style of that time. There were some clothes laid out and a mother-of-pearl handled hairbrush on a dressing table.

"Was this your mother's room?" she asked.

He shook his head. "No. This is not the Duchess's room. It was a guest room when the house was private. My father kept the actual Duke and Duchess's rooms in the private part of the house, but this room was set up to look like it. This was actually my great-grandmother's room."

"So your great-grandmother used it?"

"Yes. You could call this the Dowager's room. Anyway, the trust decided to set this room up as the Duchess's room for the tours. These are just smaller than the actual rooms they represent." He opened the door. "This is the door that leads to the Duke's room."

"So he could visit the Duchess at night." Then her cheeks heated as she realized what she'd just said.

He smiled at her lazily and took a step toward her. "Why, yes, if they wanted the bloodline to continue, that is."

"I... I suppose so." Geri found it hard to breathe at the moment, standing so close to him. She could reach out and touch him. Her pulse was thundering in her ears and before she could stop what she wanted to happen, Thomas's arm slipped around her and he was pulling her tight up against him, his lips capturing hers in a kiss that sent a zing of heat through her body.

She melted into him, but the moment his hand slipped down her back she knew she had to put a stop to this now before something they both regretted happened.

He broke the kiss off before she did. "I'm terribly sorry, Geraldine. I don't know what came over me."

"It's okay," she whispered, trying to regain her composure. "It's okay."

"No, it's not. I promised you I wouldn't do that."

"Thomas, let's just forget it ever happened." And that's what she wanted to do, before his kiss made her imagine something out of a historical romance novel and Thomas coming through that door on their wedding night.

It was a silly notion, but she understood why he brought women here, and then it completely sobered her that he *had* brought other women here. She refused to fall for another bad boy. She wasn't going to be seduced by someone who was going to break her heart again. She just wouldn't let that happen.

The Duke's room was darker and more masculine than the Duchess's room. She walked around it, trying to put some distance between the two of them. She couldn't help but wonder what the real rooms looked like.

The Duke's room had dark wood paneling, heavy curtains and decor in forest green or burgundy. It was very much a contrast to the Duchess's room.

"Very dark. Is that where you got your nickname?"

"Perhaps, but I didn't have a say over the decor in here. It was the style at the time."

She didn't know what else to say but she knew she had to get out of the rooms before Thomas tried to kiss her again or, worse, she tried to kiss him.

They just stood there, staring at each other, not saying a word.

Suddenly they heard a group of people talking and Thomas dashed across the room and took her hand, leading her out of the room.

"Where are we going?" she asked.

"To another room. The tour is coming and I really don't want to be seen."

"Would they even know who you were?"

He shot her a look. "They know who I am. My portrait hangs in the portrait gallery."

Now she was intrigued. "There's a portrait gallery?"

"Of course. Every good estate has one."

"Can I see it?"

"Yes," he groaned halfheartedly. He took her down the stairs to a long hallway where every Duke and Duchess of Weatherstone's portrait hung, with his own large portrait at the very end.

The portrait was painted to match all the others. In it he was dressed in a naval uniform.

"I didn't know you served in the Navy," she said.

Thomas nodded.

Geri couldn't help but stare up at the portrait. He looked so young in it. So handsome. He still was handsome, but seeing him in that uniform made her feel weak in the knees. Thomas Ashwood had hidden depths.

"Well, it's getting late," Thomas said, interrupting her thoughts. "Perhaps we should get back to London now."

"Right. Of course. Thank you for showing me your home."

"My pleasure."

"Don't forget about our arrangement."

"What arrangement was that again?" he asked.

"That you attend a Christmas function for one of your tours."

He groaned. "I thought you'd forgotten about that."

"No, I didn't forget. I plan to hold you to it."

"Well, as long as you plan to attend my special Christmas appearance. I mean, it wouldn't be a traditional Weatherstone Christmas with just the Duke by himself."

"But I'm not a Duchess," she said, and then she realized what she'd just said and felt completely mortified.

A strange look passed across his face. "No. I guess you're not."

"No, I'm not."

And she never would be.

CHAPTER TWELVE

THOMAS STOOD IN the MRI lab, waiting for Charles's scans to come up. He stood next to Dr. Hunyadi, who was the radiologist at Meadowgate Hospital. Dr. Hunyadi was a bit put out to be called down to assess the scans, but with an angiosarcoma you couldn't always wait.

"Really, Mr. Ashwood, I can look at these later and diagnose it. You don't have to be here."

Thomas shook his head. "There's no need to diagnose it. We know what he has. I just need to see how much it's grown. I need to see these scans now. This patient is very important."

Thomas didn't really have any privileges at Meadowgate Hospital, but Charles was insistent that everything take place here, where he was getting his chemo. He did not want to be recognized and pitied at the hospital where they all worked. Which was silly, and Thomas had told him that.

Dr. Hunyadi just shook his head and Thomas ignored him. He watched Charles in the MRI tube, waiting for the scans of the heart to be produced. He wanted to see how far it had progressed since the last scan, because angiosarcomas of the heart were one of the fastest growing and rarest tumors. He wanted to make sure it hadn't spread into Charles's lungs yet, because if it spread into his lungs it was going to make surgery even more difficult.

The image began to load. Thomas leaned over the technician to watch, holding his breath as if that would have any impact on what was going on in Charles's body.

The angiosarcoma was small, thankfully, and he breathed an inward sigh of relief to see it. It hadn't spread, which made Thomas even happier, but it was still there and it still needed to come out or it would grow until Charles's heart failed.

There was some free fluid buildup around his heart, which would make things trickier. If it hadn't been for the routine scan for his stomach cancer they would never have found this angiosarcoma. Usually they were discovered when it was too late, as angiosarcomas didn't have any obvious symptoms.

When they were found it was sometimes mistaken for congestive heart failure, where symptoms were fluid around the heart and pain like angina. Even before those symptoms set in Charles could've formed an embolism that would've blocked a blood vessel and put him at risk of a stroke or sudden death.

Either way, having this angiosarcoma was dangerous to Charles, and Thomas was going to do everything in his power to save him for Geraldine's sake. To give her a chance to make amends with her father. A chance he himself had never got. A chance he'd never taken and something he regretted.

"That's a nasty angiosarcoma," Dr. Hunyadi said.

"I've seen worse," Thomas said. "Much worse."

"Still," Dr. Hunyadi said, "it's going to be difficult to get clear margins."

Thomas nodded. "I know."

And then and there that he wanted to do the surgery at the hospital where he had privileges. Their hospital. He didn't want to do it here. He wanted his scrub nurse, his tools, his team of surgeons, nurses and anesthesiologists. People he trusted to help him.

He wanted the operating theater he was comfortable in. That way he could do the most effective surgery and save Charles's life for now because even if he could get most of the angiosarcoma out there was no way he could get 100 percent of it out with a really clean border.

It was something they would have to monitor and do several surgeries on until they couldn't any longer.

He was going to have to try to convince Charles to give up his pride and vanity and have the surgery done at the proper place. And he would have to keep Geraldine away or he would have to convince Charles to tell his daughter what was actually going on. She had a right to know.

Just like he'd had the right to know about Zoe.

The tech went and took Charles out of the scanner and took out the IV filled with the contrast fluid that had been pumping through his veins so Thomas could get a look at the angiosarcoma.

"Have them sent to my office," Thomas said, handing Dr. Hunyadi his business card.

Dr. Hunyadi nodded and pocketed the card. "I will. Are you going to be doing the surgery here?"

"Why?" Thomas asked.

"I would like to observe it. I have never seen an angiosarcoma removal done before and I would like to watch."

"If Lord Collins allows you to, which I'm sure he will. He is all for education."

"Lord Collins?" Dr. Hunyadi said. "You mean the Lord Collins who is a cardiologist?"

"Yes," Thomas said.

"He was the cardiologist for my mother. He's an amazing doctor."

Thomas nodded. "He is...or he was. He's not practicing anymore."

"Who's taking over his practice?"

"His daughter." Thomas ended the conversation. He didn't really want to talk about it anymore. He didn't want to talk about Geraldine at this moment because he felt incredibly guilty about her not knowing about her father's condition.

And when he thought about her, he couldn't get that kiss out of his head.

He'd promised her that he wouldn't put any moves on her at his estate. Yes, he had taken other women there for that sole purpose in his younger days, when he'd been foolish. But in recent years he had avoided going there because when he walked through those halls all he could think about was his lonely childhood and the family he would never have.

And then he was reminded of his beloved mother and the brother he was supposed to have had.

He was reminded of his father's bitterness and loneliness, but seeing it through Geraldine's eyes had put it a new light. And he couldn't help but pull her into his arms and kiss her, like he'd always wanted to. He was falling for her. Though he didn't want to.

Don't think about her right now.

He had to put her out of his mind because he was with her father and he was about to discuss her father's cancer with him.

"Well?" Charles asked when Thomas walked into the room.

Thomas shook his head. "It's not good."

Charles sighed. "How much as it grown?"

"Just a little bit. A millimeter, but it's only been a few days since your last scan. So it's growing rapidly. I need to get in there and get it out."

Charles nodded. "Well, I'm ready. I'm sure I can get an operating theater set up here—"

"No," Thomas said, cutting him off. "I can't do the surgery here. I want my team with me."

Charles began to argue, but Thomas cut him off again. "You're not a surgeon, Charles. You're a damn fine cardiologist. You've shown me so much that I won't ever be able to repay you for, but a surgeon needs familiarity when tackling an insurmountable challenge."

"Are you saying my tumor is insurmountable?" Charles teased.

"Well, as you know, it's almost impossible to get every last bit of an angiosarcoma out. There's no way to leave clean margins in a heart."

"I know," Charles said. "I don't even care anymore if other people know at our hospital, it's Geraldine I'm concerned about."

"Why don't you tell her? You promised me if I took her to the garden party you'd tell her."

"Tell her what? That I'm dying? She knows that."

"Tell her about the angiosarcoma. People pull through stomach cancer all the time. That's what she believes. Yes, you have stomach cancer. I could see the tumor in your stomach on the MRI. It's been responding well to the chemotherapy since your last scan. You could beat stomach cancer, but this angiosarcoma... You're in for a lot of surgeries. Chemotherapy is weakening your body. The medication you're on is weakening your body. You could suffer from neutropenia, blood loss, pneumonia. Your body is about to be put through the wringer and you want me to cut open your chest and take apart your heart in a hospital I'm not familiar with. I'm not comfortable doing that, Charles. I need to be where I'm comfortable."

Charles looked sullen, but Thomas knew in that moment that Charles understood. That he had been beaten.

"Well, maybe I'll get someone else to do it."

Thomas saw the twinkle in Charles's eyes and knew

he was teasing him. "And who else are you going to get to do it? Who else is better than me? I'm the top cardio-thoracic surgeon in London. You know how many people I've worked on?"

"I know, I know."

"And who better to do surgery than a duke?" Thomas teased.

Charles groaned and rolled his eyes. "Just as arrogant as your father."

"And don't you love it."

"All right, all right," Charles said. "I'll have the surgery done at our hospital. Today?"

Thomas nodded. "If I can do it today."

"I want it done today. The sooner the better. I don't want Geraldine to know."

"That's up to you, but you're backing out on our deal. You said I could tell her if you didn't," Thomas said. "So if she asks me I'm not hiding anything from her."

"You're my doctor. Doctor-patient confidentiality."

"You're also my friend. I shouldn't even be doing this surgery. You're my mentor and I think of you like a father. You know that, don't you?"

Charles was silent, at a loss for words. "Thank you."

"So are you going to tell Geraldine?"

"If I have to."

"It's not if you have to," Thomas said. "You should. Open up to her, Charles."

"How can I open up to her when she won't open up to me? She hates me."

"I don't think she hates you."

"Maybe not hate, but she's not warm to me. We're not friends. I'm just a housemate."

"What do you expect, Charles? She lived without know-ing who her father was for most of her life and then you just show up out of the blue."

"I didn't know she existed until last year. Her mother never told me she was pregnant. Her mother left me. I was brokenhearted. I never for once thought that when she left she was carrying Geraldine. If I had known I was going be a father I would've done something much sooner. I always wanted a child."

"You're telling the wrong person," Thomas said. "Tell Geraldine. Tell her before it's too late."

"Promise me something, Thomas."

His stomach sank, because he knew what Charles was going to ask him and he wasn't sure that he was able to give a promise.

"What do you need, Charles?"

"Take care of Geraldine for me. If I die, please take care of her. She has no one else."

And though he shouldn't, he nodded. "I promise."

Though he wasn't sure he was the right person to do that. How could he promise to take care of someone when his own future was so uncertain?

"You know that Christmas is only a few days away, my dear."

"I do know that, Lord Twinsbury," Geri said. He was trying everything to get her to discharge him. Only she couldn't. Thomas had to.

He *tsked* under his breath. "I told you to call me Lionel. Lord Twinsbury makes me feel ancient."

"You're not ancient," Geri said. "You're pretty spritely for seventy-three."

Lord Twinsbury groaned. "Oh, when you say that, I feel even older."

"My apologies. Now hold still so I can take your blood pressure."

"The nurse has just done that."

"Nonetheless," Geri chastised him as she wrapped the

band around Lord Twinsbury's arm and hit the button. The machine flashed a blood pressure figure that was stable but still not the best.

"How is it?" Lord Twinsbury asked.

"Stable, but you'll be in here over Christmas."

"I have never missed the King's College carols."

"I'm sorry to disappoint you, but this time you will. Your health is important."

"Stuff and nonsense."

Geri shook her head. "Lie back and try to rest. I hear you've been giving the nurses grief."

Lord Twinsbury grinned. "I don't think so."

"Behave—that's a warning." Geri picked up her chart and left his room. When she turned the corner of the intensive care unit she saw that Thomas was waiting at the end of the hall. He didn't smile at her when he saw her.

I knew it. I knew that kiss was going to make things awkward for us.

She approached him, but he still didn't smile at her in the way he usually did, and she had a sinking feeling that something had happened.

"Is it Zoe?" she asked.

"No. Zoe is fine. It's something else."

"Thomas, I thought we agreed not to talk about that kiss again," she said under her breath.

A funny expression crossed his face. "What?"

"I don't want it to affect our business relationship."

Thomas scrubbed his hand over his face. "It's not that."

"What is it, then?"

"Your father."

The blood drained from her face, but she kept her composure. "What about him?"

"He's been admitted here and he's having surgery tomorrow. He would have surgery today, but there isn't an operating theater available."

"Oh, is that all?"

Thomas frowned. "What do you mean, is that all?"

"I take it it's about his stomach cancer. Who is doing the surgery?"

Thomas grabbed her by the shoulders. "It's not the stomach cancer. He's on this floor, at the end of the hall. Go and see him. He'll explain."

Before she could grill him further about it he walked away from her.

Geri shook her head and headed down the hall. Thomas was right, her father was there. A nurse was finishing up his vitals and he was in his pajamas, an IV started already.

"Is everything okay here?" Geri asked, confused.

"Just finishing the preoperative workup, Dr. Collins," the nurse said cheerfully.

"Preoperative workup?"

"Yes, Mr. Ashwood asked for it." The nurse finished up and left the room.

"What was she talking about?" Geri asked finally. "What does she mean, Mr. Ashwood has asked for a preoperative workup?"

"Just exactly that, Geraldine. I'm going in for surgery tomorrow," Charles said.

"Tomorrow? You're supposed to have chemotherapy tomorrow."

"It's been postponed. Thomas and my oncologist agree that this is the best course of treatment for the moment."

"To cut the stomach cancer out?" She was confused.

"No, my angiosarcoma."

The world began to spin as the words began to sink in. She knew exactly what that was and the thought of the father she just found having it made her angry.

"Geraldine, I know this isn't ideal—"

"Well, of course not. It's serious, but at least you're getting it dealt with." She couldn't deal with this. She'd just found her father and now he might die tomorrow. She had to get out of there. "I'll let you rest. You have a big day tomorrow."

"Geraldine…"

She ignored him and left his room. There were so many emotions going through her. Ones she couldn't even process. She just knew that she had to put distance between herself and her father.

A father who was about to abandon her again.

She grabbed her purse and coat from the doctors' lounge and headed out into the street. It was snowing lightly, but instead of enjoying it, like she usually did, she kept her head down and walked. She had every intention of returning to Harley Street and throwing herself into her work.

When she kept herself busy she didn't have to feel anything.

It numbed unwelcome feelings.

Only she didn't head back to Harley Street. She wandered around Knightsbridge for a few hours and then, instead of heading to Holland Park, she found herself standing in front of Thomas's Notting Hill home. She didn't know if he was home or not, but she tried the buzzer.

"Yes?" Thomas sounded agitated.

"It's me, Geraldine. Can I come in?"

"Yes," he said quickly. He buzzed the gate open and as she walked up the path he met her outside. "I've been looking all over for you."

"Why?" she asked.

"Your father said you were in a daze when he broke the news. I was worried so I went to the office, but Mrs. Smythe said you hadn't been in, and then I went to Holland Park. I was about to go back to the hospital and start over again."

"I just went for a walk. I'm fine."

No. I'm not.

Only she wasn't sure how she was processing this information.

"I don't think you are. Come inside where it's warmer." When she was inside she began to shiver and he helped her out of her coat. "You must be chilled to the bone, walking from the hospital to here. That's a long walk."

"It didn't feel like a long walk until this moment." She kicked off her shoes, her feet feeling like blocks of ice because she'd been wearing a skirt and stockings instead of slacks.

Thomas wrapped an arm around her. His body heat felt good and she snuggled up against him, shivering, while he rubbed her shoulders. Then before she had a moment to protest he scooped her up in his arms and carried her upstairs, but not to the sitting room where they had been the night before.

"Where are we going?"

"My room is the warmest. I have a gas fire going in there. Zoe was in there earlier today, but she's gone over to a friend's house for the night."

A blush crept up her neck. "Why don't we go to the sitting room?"

"Because it's being cleaned. Now, stop fidgeting so I can carry you upstairs properly."

Thomas took her to his bedroom at the top of the stairs. It was a large room and there was a sitting area, where a gas fireplace was giving off heat. He set her down on the couch and tucked a blanket around her. Geri could see he had been working. Spread out on a coffee table were scans and medical journals.

"I was doing some research, brushing up on my surgical skills and hoping I can find something that would benefit your father's surgery tomorrow."

Geri picked up the MRI scan and stared at the angiosarcoma in her father's heart. Like a monster, eating away at him. She set it down quickly.

"I'm sorry for interrupting your work. I just didn't want to be alone right now."

Thomas sat down next to her. "I don't blame you. It's a scary thing."

"It'll be impossible for you get to good margins. When I was doing my residency as a surgeon…" Then she realized what she'd been saying and the floodgates opened. She couldn't hide it anymore. Was tired of hiding it.

She was a surgeon in her heart.

She missed it and because of her training she knew what had to happen to her father and it terrified her.

"You were going to be a surgeon. I knew it."

"Yes."

"Why did you stop?"

Tears stung her eyes. "I fell in love with the wrong man, my teacher, and I thought he loved me, but… I was a fool. So I walked away from surgery and it was then I discovered I had a father and he was offering me a practice far away from Glasgow. Far away from Frederick. I ran away from my problems."

"You're not the only one," Thomas said.

"I'm not?"

"I have hypertrophic cardiomyopathy. Or at least the genetic traits for it. I ran from any form of happiness, because there's no guarantee I won't die prematurely as well."

Geri ran a hand through her hair and leaned back against the couch. "We're a right pair of loons, aren't we?"

Thomas chuckled and then reached out, his hand on her knee. "He'll be okay."

His simple touch felt so good and she recalled the way it had felt to be in his arms. How safe he'd made her feel. How good that kiss had been. She just wanted to forget everything. For once she wanted to not think about every consequence and throw caution to the wind once more.

To taste passion again.

It might not mean anything, because she was too afraid to feel love again, but she wanted to be with Thomas, wanted the Dark Duke to seduce her. She didn't want to feel at the moment, just wanted to taste passion and give in to the temptation.

She leaned over and kissed Thomas on the lips, catching him off guard, but only for a moment, and then he was kissing her back. This was what she wanted. She just wanted to feel this moment with him.

"Geraldine," he said huskily. "I don't want to ruin anything…"

"You won't." She wrapped her hand around his neck. "This doesn't have to mean anything. Please, just stay with me. Be with me."

Thomas gave in with a groan and took her in his arms and carried her over to his large bed across the room. Her pulse was racing with anticipation over what was going to happen, because she wanted this to happen. And she wanted it to be Thomas to erase the memories of Frederick.

To make her not feel anything.

She just wanted to be herself again.

They sank onto the mattress together, kissing. She didn't want any part of them separated. She just wanted to feel him pressed against her. No words were needed, because she knew that at this moment they both wanted the same thing. The kiss ended and they began to undress each other, slowly, kissing in between because they didn't want to break the connection of their lips.

Geri knew if they stopped for too long it might not happen.

And she wanted it to happen.

"I wanted to kiss you the moment I met you," Thomas whispered against her cheek. "I wanted you."

"I wanted you to kiss me too." She was terrified because the last time she had been this vulnerable to somebody, he'd broken her heart. Only she hadn't given her heart to Thomas, so there was no way he could break it.

Are you sure?

She shook that thought out of her head and let herself be vulnerable to him. There was no point in questioning the inevitable. She wanted this. Only under Thomas's smoldering gaze she suddenly felt a bit embarrassed about being naked in front of him. That she was so exposed to him.

"You don't need to hide from me," he said, as if sensing her apprehension.

They lay next to each other, both exposed and naked. She couldn't get enough of touching him, feeling his muscles ripple under her fingertips, running her hands over his skin and through his hair, but the most heady feeling was having his strong hands on her.

"I haven't been with anyone since Frederick," she admitted, embarrassed.

He tipped her chin so she was looking at him. "Don't be embarrassed." He kissed her again, his lips urgent as he pulled her body flush with his.

This was it.

This was the moment. He pressed her against the mattress. His hands entwined with hers, his body so large over hers, she felt safe.

Thomas gave her a kiss that seared her very soul. The warmth spread through her veins and then his lips moved from her mouth down her neck, following the erratic pulse points under her skin.

Geri couldn't ever remember feeling this way before. Not with anyone else. There was something different about this.

"I want you so much," she said, and she was surprised at herself for being so vocal about her desire, her need to have him possess her. She felt free. Her whole life had been about control. It had been the only way to keep the feelings out, to muddle through each day. The only way to cope with a life that had dealt with her harshly.

His body shifted.

"Where are you going?" she asked in a daze.

"To get protection. I didn't get it sooner because I couldn't think clearly with you kissing me like that."

He moved away and got protection. When he came back she trembled in his arms.

"Don't be nervous," he said.

"I'm not." And that was the truth. She wasn't nervous, but she could feel the tremendous amount of emotion welling up inside her.

He stroked her cheek and kissed her gently again. His lips gently nipped at her mouth, his hand on her breast and the other touching her between her legs. Desire coursed through her, was overwhelming. No man had ever made her feel this way before.

Not even Frederick, who she'd thought had been her most passionate love affair, but then Frederick had said she was always cold between the sheets.

"I know you want me," Thomas whispered huskily.

"I do."

He kissed her deeply as he entered her. She cried out in the pleasure of him taking her, because she couldn't ever recall feeling like this before. He was so deep. She wrapped her legs around his legs, urging him to go even deeper. To take all of her.

To completely possess her.

She felt so alive. So free in that moment.

Nothing existed but the two of them locked together in a passionate embrace. She wanted him completely as he thrust in her. It wasn't long before both of them released, close together, in shared pleasure.

When it was over he rolled on his back, holding her tight against him. She could hear his heart racing in time with hers. She'd never expected it to be like this with him. Of course she'd never expected it to be like anything with him, but the more time she'd spent with him the more she'd felt the ice around her heart thawing. The more she felt the control on her emotions slip away, the more alive she felt.

And it frightened her, because she didn't know anything else but heartache and pain.

CHAPTER THIRTEEN

THOMAS COULDN'T BELIEVE what had just happened. When he'd first seen Geraldine he'd been attracted to her, there was no doubt about it, and he'd thought about seducing her. Though he'd grown tired of that game. The chase and seduction. His reputation as the Dark Duke. He'd still wanted Geraldine. He just hadn't had any intention of pursuing it further, because there was no further for him.

Once he'd learned she was Charles's daughter and his new partner she had become off-limits. He'd never thought this day would come. He had been going to make sure this wouldn't happen.

Even with Charles's blessing.

When they'd grown closer, he'd often fantasized about holding her in his arms, just like this, because even though he'd sworn he would never let this happen, he had desired her. The more he'd got to know her, the more he'd enjoyed being in her company, the more he'd wanted her.

Since his father's death and his diagnosis he'd had affair after affair, seducing women and not thinking any more about them afterwards, but he realized now it had never been like this with anyone. Not even Cassandra, who had been his longest relationship.

Usually those seductions had taken place at their place or in a hotel. Even once in a cloakroom closet. This was the first time he'd brought someone into his home, to his room and his bed, and made love to them.

It had been so long since he'd made love to anyone.

This was something different and it scared him.

There were so many emotions churning inside him. Lying here next to Geraldine was something totally different and for one moment he got an inkling of what his father had felt for his mother.

It scared him to think of losing Geraldine because it would crush him.

No. This isn't love. It can't be.

Geraldine didn't love him. She just needed him. She was going through something emotionally overwhelming. This was just about sating the desire they both had for each other. There had been no promises made. She'd made that clear. She just wanted him at this moment and he couldn't let his heart open again. Not even to her.

Why?

He looked down at her against the pillow, her honey-brown hair fanning around her head like a halo, her body relaxed. Everything he'd just told himself seemed just like an excuse, because what he'd thought would only take once to get her out of his system made him realize that he needed more of her.

He wanted more of her. And that scared him.

As if she knew he was looking at her she opened her eyes and smiled up at him. A pink tinge flushed those creamy white cheeks.

"Sorry, I drifted off."

"It's quite all right," he said. "I'm sorry for disturbing you. You must be exhausted."

"Not totally exhausted." She smiled and then sat up. She got out of bed and picked up her clothes, pulling them on.

"What're you doing?" he asked.

"Getting dressed. I should probably get home."

"Don't you want to go to the hospital and see your father?"

She shrugged. "I saw him."

"Do you not care that your father is going to be going through this major surgery tomorrow?"

"You're the surgeon. You'll do a good job."

"Yes, but usually when people's loved ones go through surgeries like this—"

She cut him off. "There's a difference, though. He may be my father biologically but I don't know him well enough to feel the emotion you're expecting from me."

He was shocked by her cold words. "He cares about you."

"He has a funny way of showing it. He's never really gone out of his way to show me that he cares. I mean, was he even going to tell me about this angiosarcoma? He's always so secretive. He went to a hospital across town to have chemotherapy."

"No," he sighed.

"Don't loved ones usually tell their family about surgeries like that?" she asked testily.

"He didn't want you to be upset."

She gave him a disbelieving look and began to pull on her clothing. "This is the way he's always been. When he introduced himself to me last year, he said, 'Hello, my name is Charles Collins and I'm your father.' He's so formal. I don't know what he expects from me. He was never there when I needed him."

"He didn't know that you existed."

"Why are you telling me this, Thomas?" she snapped. "He should be the one telling me this."

"You're absolutely right. He should be the one telling you this. Go to him."

"Would you stop pushing my father on me? I don't need him. Just like every man in my life, he was never there when I needed him. He never supported me, he abandoned me. You should know about abandonment. Look what your father did to you."

It was like a slap across the face, but she was right.

"You're right."

"I think I'd better go," Geraldine whispered.

"Yes. Go and run away from your problems again," he snapped.

What he'd said was like a knife through the heart, when he'd told her that she was running again. Because that's exactly what she was doing, but saying it out loud stung all the more because he knew that she was vulnerable.

She didn't like feeling vulnerable.

When Frederick had made her feel this way, she'd run away from him and given up her dream of being a surgeon.

The one time she'd taken a chance and let a man in when she'd told herself not to she'd been hurt again. Thomas had hurt her.

"You don't know what you're saying," she said. "You haven't been through what I've been through."

He shook his head. "How can you say that? I've told you about my childhood. My father was bitter. He lost my mother and unborn baby brother and that was it for him. He was done. I was just a reminder of the woman he loved. He didn't want me around. At least your mother loved you."

"That's where you're wrong," she said. "My mother didn't love me. I was a nuisance. I cramped her lifestyle. I don't know why she didn't send me off to live with my father, but she never did. She liked to remind me I was a burden, a mistake. I was alone most of my childhood."

"That is no reason to run away from your father now. Make it right."

"You don't know anything," she snapped. "It's my life. I didn't ask you to be a part of it."

His spine stiffened and his face was like thunder. "Is that how it's going to be, then?"

"Yes," she said.

"Fine." He turned his back to her, closing her out, and she knew she'd ruined her chance with him. She knew she'd ruined everything and there was no going back, but Thomas didn't know what he was talking about. He was meddling where he shouldn't.

She couldn't make up with her father. The anger she carried for him was still there, although buried. She'd been alone for so long. She didn't know how to be anything else but alone.

Maybe you didn't realize how lonely you were.

"I'm not the only one running away, you know. You use your father and your heart condition as an excuse to run from any kind of attachment. To push people away. You're no better than me. You just don't want to admit it."

He didn't acknowledge her.

Stubborn.

She let herself out of Thomas's home and wandered down the street towards Holland Park. She only walked for a bit until she decided to take a taxi back to her father's home.

She just had to put it all out of her mind. She shouldn't have slept with Thomas. That had been a huge mistake. They were supposed to be just business partners. That was it, but she'd let him through her barriers. He'd made her feel and having emotions that weren't controlled was a dangerous thing indeed.

As she walked into her father's home it was empty. Strangely empty. Even though there had been times over the past couple of months that her father had been working or out with friends he had always come home.

Her mother would go out sometimes and not return for days.

She'd gotten used to having someone around. She just hadn't realized it until now, in this moment. She'd gotten used to his presence without even knowing it. Wandering into the sitting room, she walked around aimlessly, staring at all the photographs of family members she didn't know and who had been long gone before she'd ever come into the picture. Pictures of her father when he'd been young. Then she saw it. A picture she'd never noticed before.

A picture of him and her mother. Happy.

She picked up the frame and felt something taped to the back. It was a letter that was marked "Return to sender." It was from her father to her mother and was addressed to her mother's home in Glasgow, the home she'd grown up in, but scrawled in red ink on the front of the envelope was, "Moved, no longer lives here."

Which had not been true.

Geri set the letter back down because it was not her business to read it, but she couldn't help herself. She opened the letter and read what the words said. Tears began to stream down her face as she realized the letter had been sent just before she was born.

And her father was begging her mother to come back to him. How much he loved her. How he didn't care that she wasn't part of his social class. He wanted to be with her, only her, and that there would be nobody else.

Which was true. Her father had never remarried. Or had another romance.

Why did her mother send the letter back? If she had just opened this letter...

Geri shook her head. No, her mother had never loved her father. She'd made that clear. She had no interest in him, or Geraldine for that matter.

As she looked in the mirror above the mantel she didn't see much of her mother in herself, but she did see her father. His eyes, the color of his hair back then, his mannerisms, and she realized that he too had shut out emotions.

Lived without feeling.

And she realized that she was throwing away the opportunity to get to know her father. Maybe if she gave him half a chance she would know what it was like to have a parent love her. She decided she was going to go to the hospital and make things right.

She had to make it right with her father.

Thomas was still fuming over his fight with Geraldine, but really what had he expected? He knew better than to dabble in the affairs of the heart.

Perhaps she is hurt too.

He shook that thought out of his head as he marched into the hospital in the middle of the night and headed up to see Charles.

He had to swallow all his emotions at the moment. He couldn't let them interfere right now, because he respected Charles too much to let him know what had just happened. His feelings aside, he had to work with Geraldine in a professional capacity. And he planned to keep it that way.

No matter what his emotions were telling him.

Charles was sitting up in bed. Pensive.

"Charles?" Thomas said, unwinding his scarf as he came into the room.

"An operating theater has become available. I want you to do the surgery. I am prepared for it. I've fasted. I'm ready."

Thomas scrubbed a hand over his face. "Are you certain?"

Charles nodded. "I am. It's growing too fast and I need it out. Or as much as you can get out."

"Have you spoken to Geraldine about this?"

"I tried to call her a moment ago, but there was no answer."

Not surprising.

Geraldine had made it quite clear that she didn't have much affection for her father and he wondered if she had any emotions at all.

"Do you still want to proceed with the surgery or shall we wait until you get hold of Geraldine?"

"No, there is no point of waiting. She'd approve."

"Yes."

Geraldine wouldn't want this surgery not to take place. Detached as she was from her father, she was logical when it came to medicine.

"If you're sure."

Charles looked at him sternly. "Very sure."

Thomas nodded. It would take a couple of hours for him to get his team ready and to call in his favorite scrub nurse, who he had no doubt would come in and assist him in this surgery as she was fond of Charles as well.

He was uneasy about operating on Charles when nothing was settled between him and his daughter, but what choice did he have? Charles was his patient and insisted on having the surgery done.

It was also in Charles's best interests to attend to the angiosarcoma as quickly as possible. He walked into the surgeons' locker room and began to change out of his street clothes. He tried to focus solely on the surgery that was about to take place, like he would do for any other patient. The only difference this time was he couldn't help but think of Geraldine.

The hurt it would cause her if her father died before she had made peace with him. It was something he had to bear daily.

Charles might not survive this surgery. Something the

three of them were all aware of, but they hadn't spoken to each other about. After he was in his scrubs he grabbed Charles's file and went over the angiosarcoma images. He closed his eyes and tried to picture it in the heart, planning where he would cut and how he would he would attack it.

"Mr. Ashwood?"

Thomas turned to see his scrub nurse, Margaret, standing there.

"Yes, Madge?"

"Dr. Collins is in the operating theater and ready."

Thomas nodded. "Thank you, Madge. I'll be there in a moment. Take the scans and make sure they're loaded somewhere I can see them."

"Of course, Mr. Ashwood."

Margaret left and Thomas closed the file. He put on his scrub cap and readied himself to head to the operating theater.

"Where is he?"

Thomas turned around to see Geraldine and even though it had only been a few hours and she had hurt him so much, his heart skipped a beat. She looked done in, apprehensive, by the way she was wringing her hands. He'd never seen her like this before.

"Your father is in the operating theater and being put under at the moment."

Geraldine worried her bottom lip. "You're going to do the surgery now?"

"I am. A theater became available and your father was insistent on it being done now."

She nodded. "He didn't call me."

"He did. You weren't…home."

A flush tinged her cheeks, because only a couple hours ago they'd been together and then the unpleasantness had occurred. The argument that still stung.

"I need to speak with him."

Thomas shook his head. "I wish I could allow that, but you know that's not possible. He's being put under general anesthesia and I can't have you contaminate the sterile field."

"But I—"

"You what?" Thomas snapped.

Tears stung her eyes and she brushed them away quickly. "It can wait."

Of course it could.

He was hoping she was going to show some kind of emotion. Admit that she cared for her father. Cared for something. Even cared for him. But instead she stood there with no expression on her face. Just a few tears.

"I have to go now."

He turned his back on her.

"Thomas?"

He turned around.

"Please. Save him." It was sincere. She was asking for another chance, the chance he'd never got with his father, and his heart melted.

He couldn't help but smile at her and he did something that he'd never done in his entire career as a surgeon. "I promise."

And he hoped that he could keep his promise to her.

He planned to keep that promise to her. He would make sure Charles pulled through this surgery.

As he scrubbed in he couldn't help but think of the chance he hadn't had with his father to say what he'd felt. How he'd hated that he had been isolated as a child after his mother had died. How his father had resented him.

How lonely he'd felt.

How he'd needed his father, but had never had one.

Even Zoe hadn't really had their father, though he'd tolerated her more, but she had been so young when their father had died. She didn't have the same feelings of disconnection or resentment that he had. Instead, he'd stepped up to be the father theirs had never been.

Charles had wanted to be a father, but had been denied that chance and Geraldine wasn't giving it to him. Wasn't allowing him to be a father. So he was damn well going to make sure that Charles pulled through so that there was a chance for them.

When he entered the operating theater he was gowned and gloved. His instruments were ready and Margaret was waiting for him.

Charles was under general and everything was ready to go.

He took a calming breath and closed his eyes. He emptied his mind of everything. Including Geraldine. All he could see was the heart, the organ he knew so well, visualized for him in his mind.

And he thought of where the angiosarcoma lay.

He knew where to begin the point of attack.

"Scalpel."

Margaret handed him the scalpel and he went to work. As he worked he could feel he was being watched and glanced up at the gallery. He didn't think that anyone would be in there because it was the middle of the night, but Geraldine was there. Standing, watching pensively.

He nodded at her in acknowledgment.

And she returned the nod.

Even though she shouldn't be watching her father undergoing this surgery he knew there was no way she was going to budge. Geraldine was here for the long haul.

As was he.

He turned his attention back to Charles and put Geraldine out of his mind. He told himself she wasn't even there, because right now he had to stay focused. He was going to save his friend, his mentor. The man who was a bit of a father figure to him. If he failed in this endeavor he knew all would be lost with Geraldine. Even though she'd hurt him deeply with her words, she'd been right to say them. Just as she'd run from surgery, he too had run from finding any kind of happiness. From allowing any kind of love to enter his heart, using the excuse of his father and a genetic condition to decide his destiny.

They were the same, try as he may to deny it in his own mind. He was in love with Geraldine Collins, because she saw him for who he really was when he couldn't even see it himself.

CHAPTER FOURTEEN

"Dr. Collins?"

Geraldine woke with a start, her body cramped because she'd been curled up in a chair in the gallery. The last thing she remembered was watching Thomas performing surgery on her father. It had been a long surgery, as most heart surgeries of this nature were. They had been trying to remove a tumor that was growing inside her father's heart.

She'd watched for as long as she could, all the while praying her father would pull through.

Geri had watched as Thomas's hands had worked so diligently to save her father.

To give her a second chance of knowing her father. There was beauty in Thomas's surgical skill, the way he moved. She hoped one day to return to the operating theater herself. She had to stop running. She had to try again.

Thomas had been working so hard to save her father when she had treated him so poorly. And when she'd been standing in her father's home last night, staring at the words he'd written to her mother, she'd realized that she was doing exactly the same thing as her mother had done to her father. She had been pushing him away.

Geri had never thought she was like her mother. She'd striven so hard not to be like her mother, yet she was.

When it came to matters of the heart she was just as cold and emotionless as her mother was.

She'd come to the hospital to make amends and when she'd seen her father wasn't in his room, it had been more than she could bear. And she'd been worried that she'd missed her chance. So she'd begged Thomas to make a promise she knew it was impossible to keep, because one never knew when doing a surgery of this nature. It was a promise surgeons didn't make to patients, yet he'd looked down at her, his expression soft, and he'd made her that promise.

"I promise."

Thomas's words ran through her head during the surgery and she'd closed her eyes, praying that she would be given a chance to right the wrongs she'd done.

She'd blown it with Thomas, but if her father pulled through there was a chance that she could make it right with him. Geri swore she would make it right.

"Dr. Collins, the surgery ended an hour ago."

"What time is it?" Geri asked the nurse who had come to wake her.

"It's seven in the morning. There's a class of medical students coming in and they need the gallery. They're going to view a cholecystectomy."

She got up. "I'm so sorry. I didn't mean to delay the surgery."

The nurse smiled. "It's quite all right. You haven't delayed anything."

"Where is my father?" she asked with some trepidation.

"He's in the intensive care unit."

Relief washed over her. "He survived?"

The nurse smiled. "He did."

Geri got up out of the chair and headed out of the gallery. Her body was stiff and she felt a bit like death warmed over, but she had to go and see her father. She was going to start making things right.

When she got down to the intensive care unit she paused at the door. Thomas was in the chair, charting. Her father was unconscious and pale. As if sensing her presence, Thomas looked up from his charting and stood up.

"Geraldine, are you…? How are you?" he asked. "I was wondering where you were."

"Fine. I was sleeping in the gallery."

He winced. "That sounds uncomfortable."

"It was." She worried her bottom lip. "How is my father?"

Thomas nodded. "He's good. He did very well coming off bypass."

Geraldine nodded. "Good."

"I was able to removed ninety-five percent of the tumor. The five percent that's still there is small and we'll start a very intensive chemotherapy and radiation routine. He'll probably need more surgery, but perhaps we can slow the growth of the angiosarcoma."

Tears stung her eyes. "That's…that's wonderful."

Thomas nodded. "I've finished his charting. I'll…leave you with him."

As he walked past Geraldine grabbed his hand. He glanced over his shoulder at her as she held it tight and whispered, "Thank you."

He didn't say anything, just nodded and then left the room.

Geraldine's knees knocked together and she took the chair that Thomas had just vacated. It was so quiet in the room, except for the sounds of the monitors, but she never really noticed those sounds. Those sounds were comforting to her.

Those sounds meant that her father was still alive. That she would have another chance with him. A chance to make it right and get to know him. She took her father's hand in hers and squeezed it tight.

"I read the letter," she whispered. "The one that's taped behind the picture of you and Mother. I'm sorry, I think I misjudged you."

Her father's eyes opened. Just briefly, then they met hers and lit up with recognition. He tried to open his mouth to say something, but winced.

"Don't try to speak," Geraldine said.

"How?" he croaked out.

"How did it go?"

He nodded very slightly.

"It went well. Thomas got ninety-five percent of the angiosarcoma. You'll need intensive chemotherapy and radiation therapy, but it went well."

Her father smiled and relaxed, squeezing her hand.

"I'm sorry, Father," she whispered.

His eyes opened again, a questioning expression on his face.

"I was cold to you. I was angry with you for not being there all those years."

His expression softened and he opened his mouth, but she shook her head.

"Don't speak. Please, just let me talk. I know you didn't know about me, but that didn't matter to me. I just pushed you away, but I know... I know how Mother hurt you. You tried to reach out to her. You sent her a letter to a Glasgow address, that's where I grew up. We were there. She lied to you and me. I swore I would never be like her, but I was. I was pushing you away when you were just trying to get to know me. I don't know you, but I want to. I want a chance before it's too late. I'm so sorry, Father."

She leaned her head on his arm and let the tears pour out of her. His hand touched the back of her head, stroking her hair, and when she looked up she could see tears in his eyes too.

"I'd like that very much, Geraldine."

Geri clung to her father. She was going to make things right.

She was going to make everything right in her life, no matter how long it took.

Geraldine took a seat in Lord Twinsbury's reserved first-class train compartment. He'd graduated from Cambridge and had a long-reserved standing seat at King's College Chapel for their Festival of Nine Lessons and Carols that was held every Christmas Eve.

She hadn't particularly wanted to leave London and come to Cambridge for this, but her father and Lord Twinsbury had insisted that she attend.

"Not everyone gets a chance to attend," her father had argued. *"Lord Twinsbury is offering you one of his seats. Take the chance and go. It's spectacular."*

Her father was going to be in the hospital over Christmas. She was going to be spending Christmas morning at the hospital with him. And since she was going to be alone on Christmas Eve, she'd decided to take her father's advice and attend the Cambridge event.

Since Jensen had the night off, she was taking the train to Cambridge and planned to stay overnight at a small inn near the university. Jensen had promised to pick her up tomorrow morning because he had plans to visit her father too.

So she sat, watching the world pass outside her train window. People bustling along the platform, carrying brightly colored packages and greeting loved ones. She envied them.

Though she had her father now. And that was something. She was going to make the most of every moment they had.

"Is this seat taken?"

Geri was surprised to see Thomas standing in the doorway of Lord Twinsbury's first-class compartment. He didn't wait for her to answer and shut the door, sitting across from her.

Her heart skipped a beat, seeing him. There was so much she wanted to say to him but she didn't know how to say it. "I don't believe it's taken."

Thomas grinned. "Good."

"I thought you didn't like to come to these things?" she said as he leaned back against the seat. "I mean, this is going to be televised."

"Yes, well, I thought I would make an exception this time."

"Really?"

Thomas nodded. "Yes. It's time to start making a big deal about Christmas, I think."

"I'm very glad to hear about that." She nodded. "It's the one time of year I truly love."

"Yes. I know." He grinned. "You've made amends with your father, I see."

"I have," she said. "And with myself. I'm afraid I'm going to have to find our practice a replacement cardiologist."

"Why?" He frowned.

"I'm going to return to surgery. I'm going to be a surgeon. I only had one year left. I've let fear drive me for so long. I've pushed people out and run away when things got too hard. Just like my mother always did. I suffered for it. I wanted to be a surgeon and I really see no other choice. I want to be a surgeon."

Thomas smiled. "I'm pleased. I knew you wanted to be a surgeon."

"Yes, well, don't look so pleased with yourself."

"I think I will gloat a bit." He grinned.

"You were right about it all and I'm… I'm sorry for the things I said. I was completely wrong about you."

"No, you weren't," he said, and she was confused.

"Of course I was."

"No, because I did the same as you. I pushed you away."

"I think we both pushed each other away," she said.

"I think I pushed the hardest. I was scared of a genetic condition that might not amount to anything. I pushed people away, afraid to suffer loss like I did as a child. I guess I didn't feel worthy enough to have love."

"You have Zoe," she whispered. "You have plenty of love."

Thomas nodded. "I do, but I don't have you."

The words caught her off guard and she wasn't sure that she'd heard him correctly. "Pardon?"

"You, Geraldine. It's you I love. You saw me for more than my title, which was all Cassandra and the women I had brief affairs with saw. My father saw me as a reminder of my mother. Only Zoe could see me for who I really was, but then you came along and you were so unimpressed by everything. All you saw me as was the surgeon. The only thing, except for my sister, I loved and had left in this world. You saw me."

"I didn't see you, Thomas. How could I when I didn't even see myself?" Her voice hitched.

"You did, though. You pushed through the walls I'd built for so long to protect myself. Just as I broke through yours." He took her hand and placed it across his chest. "You are my heart and soul. You made me realize I want to risk it all. I love you."

A tear escaped from her eye and rolled down her cheek, because there was no sense in hiding what she felt. "I was so afraid of love. No one ever loved me. I thought Frederick did, but I was wrong. I didn't know what love was until I met you. You infuriating man. I love you too."

Thomas moved beside her and touched her face gently, wiping away the tears slipping down her cheeks and kissing her in the private compartment, while people buzzed and milled about outside, trying to find their own trains or seats.

Normally this would bother her, people seeing her like this, but she didn't care as she clung to Thomas. She'd thought she'd ruined her chance with him. Her chance at love, because she'd been so afraid to chase after it.

So afraid that what had happened before would happen again.

He was, after all, a notorious seducer of women, but the only thing he seduced at this moment was her heart.

It belonged to him completely and she had to take the chance and let him hold a piece of it, damaged as it was, because she was certain that only his love could mend it, and that she would mend his as well.

"I love you, Lady Collins. I am a bit put out that you're leaving our practice high and dry without a cardiologist and I think Zoe will be most displeased that you won't be her doctor anymore, but she'll understand."

"I am sorry about that, but I'll help you find a suitable replacement. I still have a share in our practice, you know."

He nodded. "I hope you won't be returning to Glasgow to finish your surgical residency."

"No, I have too much in London to leave. I'll be doing my residency at St. Thomas Aquinas."

"Well, don't think you'll be getting any favours from the surgeon you'll be learning from. Even if you are sleeping with him." He winked.

"I wouldn't dream of it." She kissed him again. "Merry Christmas, Your Grace."

"Happy Christmas, Lady Collins."

EPILOGUE

Christmas Eve, one year later

"You're shaking," her father remarked.

Geri turned and took her father's hand as they sat in the back of her father's car on their way to Buckinghamshire, where she was marrying Thomas and becoming the Duchess of Weatherstone.

She'd wanted to spend the night before her wedding in Holland Park with her father, who was doing well, given that he was still undergoing chemotherapy. He'd lost his hair, but Geraldine had told him that it suited him.

He'd been happy to learn that she and Thomas were engaged and getting married, but he'd tried to get out of walking her down the aisle because he hadn't wanted to scare anyone with his looks. Chemotherapy was taking its toll, but he still looked quite debonair in his grey morning suit.

"I look like a billiard ball."

"No, you look like Daddy Warbucks," Thomas had teased.

"I assure you I'm nowhere near as wealthy as Daddy Warbucks," her father had groused.

"You're handsome, Father, and you'll look great walking me down the aisle."

"Are you cold?" Her father asked, concerned. "I think you should've picked a dress that was warmer."

"I think she looks great," Zoe commented from the other side of Geri's father. Zoe had insisted on spending the night before the wedding at Holland Park as well, as she was the bridesmaid.

Her father smiled at her. "You were the one who picked out the wedding gown. Did it really have to show so much skin?"

Geri laughed. "I like the dress too." And she did. It was simple but gorgeous and even though her father said it showed a lot of skin, it was covered with lace. It reminded her of the gown Grace Kelly had worn for her wedding, which had always been her favorite.

A dream dress of hers. She'd never thought she would get the chance to wear a wedding gown, but there she was, sitting in the back of her father's car, which Jensen was driving to Weatherstone House to marry Thomas.

The love of her life.

"I'm nervous, that's all. I just wanted a simple wedding."

Her father patted her hand. "You're marrying the Duke of Weatherstone. A small wedding is out of the question."

It had been a whirlwind year. She'd finished off her residency and was now a surgeon working at St. Thomas Aquinas. Thomas and her father had found a suitable cardiologist to replace her at the practice and she enjoyed working in the hospital, doing surgeries far more often than Thomas, still in the private practice.

The car turned up the long drive and Geri took a deep breath. She was terrified, but she'd never wanted anything more in her life.

She wanted Thomas and wanted to spend the rest of her life with him.

"There's press here!" Zoe exclaimed.

Geri cursed under her breath. "Why is there press here?"

"He's the Duke of Weatherstone," her father reminded her.

"What have I got myself into?" Then she laughed with her father.

"Did your mother respond to your invitation?" he asked.

"No. She won't be coming. She's on a cruise at the moment." Geri may have been able to repair relations with her father, but she doubted whether she and her mother would ever have any kind of relationship. It was clear that her mother didn't want anything more to do with her. It hurt, but Geri had long ago moved on.

Geri wasn't going to live a life like her mother's.

She was happy for the first time in a long time and she intended to keep it that way.

Jensen parked the car in front of the chapel that was in the grounds of Weatherstone. It was a small church, so by society standards their wedding *was* small. Jensen got out and opened the door to help Zoe out in her aubergine-colored bridesmaid's dress.

"Are you ready?" Charles asked.

"Yes." Her voice shook. "More than ready."

He nodded and climbed out the opposite side, waiting for her as Jensen held out his hand. She took it and he helped her out.

"My lady," Jensen said, beaming.

Geri gave him a quick peck on the cheek while Zoe fluffed out her dress. She took her father's hand and he led her up the steps, only now he was the one shaking.

"Are you all right, Father?"

He nodded and placed his top hat on his head. "I've just found you and now I'm giving you away. That town house will be quiet now."

Tears stung her eyes and she kissed her father. "I'm only a short tube ride away in Notting Hill."

Her father groaned. "The tube? Honestly? A duchess riding on the tube?"

"I'm not a duchess yet," she teased.

"You will be in a moment," he said. "Come on, then."

The doors opened and Zoe started down the aisle. Geri took a deep breath and held her father tight as he walked her in. All she could see for the first few moments was a sea of brightly colored hats. Which was overwhelming as everyone stood up. Her father took off his top hat and tucked it under his arm, while she clung to the other one.

Then she focused her attention to the end of the aisle and saw Thomas standing there in his morning suit, his hands clasped behind his back, grinning from ear to ear. When his gaze landed on her, she almost melted.

That twinkle in his eyes, the secret smile was just for her. It was hard to believe that a year ago that same smile and same twinkle had made her want to run in the opposite direction. Now she was running toward him.

She knew the vicar was saying something, but she couldn't quite hear him as her father passed her hand to Thomas and took his seat in the front pew of the church. Thomas just beamed at her and she couldn't believe how lucky she was.

Love was something she hadn't ever believed in after her mother and Frederick had toyed with her heart, but Thomas had made everything right.

The final vows were made and the rings slipped on their fingers.

"You may now kiss the bride," the vicar said.

Thomas leaned in and kissed her on the lips.

"I love you," she said, as he took her hand and led her down the aisle.

"I have a surprise for you." Thomas led her out of the chapel and across the lawn to the house.

"Why are we going in here? We have to have pictures

in the arboretum first," she said as he brought her into the main hall. The house and estate were closed to tourists today, thankfully. Thomas covered her eyes and led her inside.

"Now you can look," he said with excitement.

Geri gasped as "Christmas trees! Two of them."

There were two thirty-foot Christmas trees in the foyer, one on either side of the large staircase. They were covered in twinkling lights and brightly colored baubles that accentuated the deep cherry-red of the wood.

"What do you think?"

"It's gorgeous. You did this?"

He nodded. "Guilty."

"But you don't like Christmas trees."

"I can change my mind."

"Last year you compared them to Pomeranians, wasn't that it?"

Thomas groaned. "I did, but that was last year and this is a gift for the new Duchess."

"Oh, no," she gasped.

Thomas cocked an eyebrow. "What's wrong?"

"I'd just got used to the idea of being Lady Collins and being way down on the list of succession."

"Yes, and…?"

"Now I'm going to be a duchess, and any children we have are going to be further up the list than me."

"Children?"

She laughed. "Yes. I assume you have to continue your line."

"Can we wait a bit on the children, though?"

"Perhaps." She wrapped her arms around him. "I suppose I have to get used to being called Your Grace. No going back now."

He kissed her possessively. "No, there isn't. And just to show you there is no going back I have something else for you." He reached into his pocket and pulled out a flat velvet box.

"What is it?" She took it from him.

"As you're the Duchess of Weatherstone this belongs to you now."

Geri opened the box and gasped at the stunning diamond necklace and earrings that lay against the silk inside the box. "They're beautiful."

"They were my mother's. They're quite old." He reached into the box and pulled out the necklace. He stepped behind her and she felt the weight of the diamonds on her neck and a kiss against her pulse point after he finished clasping it. "They have been worn by every Duchess of Weatherstone since the time of James III."

"It's beautiful," Geri said, touching it. "It makes me nervous to have something so old in my possession."

"Well, if you had accepted Lord Twinsbury's proposal…"

"You're impossible."

"What do you think of your gifts?" Thomas asked as she wrapped his arms around her again.

"I love them."

"Is that all?"

"I love you too, Your Grace."

"And I you. Thank you for bringing me back to life and mending my heart."

"Thank you for mending mine." She grabbed him by the lapels of his morning coat and kissed him before the wedding guests came in to enjoy the wedding brunch.

After the brunch they would head off to Greece, to escape the winter.

"I can't wait to get you to Greece and get away from all of this."

"I thought you were a Christmas convert?" she asked.

"I am, believe me I am, but I'm looking forward to some

sunshine and spending many a hot night with you wrapped up in my arms, until we head back to reality."

"That sounds divine, Your Grace. Absolutely divine."

She'd tell him about the baby later.

* * * * *

If you enjoyed this story,
check out these other great reads from
Amy Ruttan

TEMPTING NASHVILLE'S CELEBRITY DOC
PERFECT RIVALS...
HIS SHOCK VALENTINE'S PROPOSAL
CRAVING HER EX-ARMY DOC

All available now!

MILLS & BOON®

MEDICAL ROMANCE™

THE ULTIMATE IN ROMANTIC MEDICAL DRAMA

A sneak peek at next month's titles...

In stores from 1st December 2016:

Just can't wait?
Buy our books online a month before they hit the shops!
www.millsandboon.co.uk

Also available as eBooks.

MILLS & BOON®

EXCLUSIVE EXTRACT

Paramedic Holly Jacobs knows that her night of scorching passion with Dr Daniel Chandler meant more than just lust. Playboy doc Daniel has sworn off love – but he can't resist Holly! By the time they get snowed in on Christmas Eve Daniel finds himself asking if Holly is for life, not just for Christmas!

Read on for a sneak preview of
PLAYBOY ON HER CHRISTMAS LIST
by Carol Marinelli

Holly wanted a kiss, Daniel knew, but he was also rather certain she wanted a whole lot more than that. Not just sex, but the part of himself he refused to give.

'What?' he said again, and then his face broke into a smile, as, very unexpectedly, Holly, sweet Holly, showed another side of her.

'Are you going to make me invite you in?'

'Yes.'

'You're not even going to try and persuade me with a kiss?' Holly checked.

'You want me or you don't.' Daniel shrugged. 'There's no question that I want you. But, Holly, do you get that—?'

She knew what was coming and she didn't need the warning—he had made his position perfectly clear—so she interrupted him. 'I don't need the speech.'

She just needed this.

Holly had thought his hand was moving to open the door but instead it came out of the window and to her head and pulled her face down to his.

He kissed her hard, even though she was the one standing. The stubble of his unshaven jaw was rough on her face and his tongue was straight in.

He pulled her in tight so that her upper abdomen hurt from the pressure of the open window and it was a warning, she knew, of the passion to come.

Even now she could pull back and straighten, say goodnight and walk off, but Holly was through with being cautious.

Her bag dropped to the pavement and he then released her.

Holly stared back at him, breathless, her lipstick smeared across her face, and all it made him want to do was to kiss her again.

But this was a street.

Holly bent and retrieved her bag and then walked off towards her flat. There was a roaring sound in her ears and her heart seemed to be leaping up near her throat.

Daniel closed up the car and was soon following her to the flats.

She turned the key in the main door to the flats and clipped up the concrete steps.

She could hear his heavy footsteps coming up the steps behind her as she turned and Holly almost broke into a run.

Daniel actually did!

He had thought her cute, sweet and gorgeous these past months and had done all he could not to think of her outright as sexy.

Except she was, and seriously so.

Don't miss
PLAYBOY ON HER CHRISTMAS LIST
by Carol Marinelli

Available December 2016

MILLS & BOON®

Why shop at millsandboon.co.uk?

Each year, thousands of romance readers find their perfect read at millsandboon.co.uk. That's because we're passionate about bringing you the very best romantic fiction. Here are some of the advantages of shopping at www.millsandboon.co.uk:

* **Get new books first**—you'll be able to buy your favourite books one month before they hit the shops

* **Get exclusive discounts**—you'll also be able to buy our specially created monthly collections, with up to 50% off the RRP

* **Find your favourite authors**—latest news, interviews and new releases for all your favourite authors and series on our website, plus ideas for what to try next

* **Join in**—once you've bought your favourite books, don't forget to register with us to rate, review and join in the discussions

Visit **www.millsandboon.co.uk**
for all this and more today!